White Thunder and Kokopelli

White Thunder
and Kokopelli

BOYD RICHARDSON

*Bob Mitchell
May you meet Kokopelli
as you pass through life.
Boyd Richardson*

CAMDEN COURT PUBLISHERS, INC.
SALT LAKE CITY, UTAH

CAMDEN COURT PUBLISHERS, INC.
9160 South 300 West, Suite 2
Sandy, UT 84070-2656

WHITE THUNDER & KOKOPELLI
Copyright © 1996 Boyd Richardson

All rights reserved under International and Pan-American Copyright Conventions. This includes the right to reproduce this book or portions thereof in any form whatsoever except as provided by the U.S. Copyright Law.

This is a fictional work, and as such, all characters and events portrayed in this book are fictional, and any resemblance to real people or incidents is purely coincidental.

ISBN 1-890828-02-5

First Printing June 1997

PRINTED IN THE UNITED STATES OF AMERICA.
10 9 8 7 6 5 4 3 2 1

Contents

Kokopelli ix
Eye-to-Eye with the Bobcat 1
Bark of a Coyote 11
The Hoot of an Owl 17
The Heat of the Day 29
Lean and Mean 37
Eyes as Bright as a Squirrel's Eyes 43
Medicine Feathers 57
Cat Whiskers 65
The Old Chant 75
The Ponies 81
Silver-Tip 89
The Rhythm of a Lullaby Chant 99
A Walk in the Forest 105
In For Hard Times 113
Under the Overhang 123
Excitement Was High 141
Regardless of the Drizzle 155
Outside the Firelight 165

My special thanks goes to Lynn Cody of the White Mountain Apache Tribe for reviewing this novel for its cultural correctness.

Characters

Beyolas .... village peace chief
Brown Horse .... Navajo slave
Butterfly Catcher .... Towhee's mother
Bylas .... Towhee's younger brother
Cat Whiskers .... Spanish official
Chind .... Navajo slave
Delgadito .... Spanish guard
Eskiminzin .... villager
Grandfather .... White Thunder's teacher
Kayenta .... Navajo slave
Kokopelli .... great shaman, one of the Three Nephites
Laughing Grass .... White Thunder's sister
Meatas .... father to White Thunder
Nan-Ted .... son of Shi-Be, brother to Sieber
Nantan Lupin .... married Laughing Grass
Quetzalcoatl .... Jesus Christ
Shi-Be .... warrior
Sieber .... son of Shi-Be, friend of White Thunder
Spirit-That-Moves-In-All-Things .... Holy Spirit
Towhee .... Apache girl
White Thunder .... Apache boy, narrator
Ysun .... giver of life—God

Kokopelli

He is more than a man. He is Kokopelli, whose likeness has been chiseled into sandstone, painted on walls, preserved on ancient ceramics and pottery, and remembered in sand paintings. A shaman popular with cultures worldwide, he is purported throughout the centuries to have the ability to heal others as well as have power over death. His name stems from the Hopi word *kachina*, which means "respected spirit". Kokopelli therefore means "kachina hump".

Portrayed as a hunchbacked man carrying a flute, Kokopelli has existed in various cultures since 200 A.D. and survives to this day. Some say that the hump on his back is indeed a sack, and that he started out as a *pochtecas*, a southern trader. The hump may be indicative of an age beyond forty years and his flute has long been a symbol of peace and tranquillity.

Kokopelli is found in the Anasazi and Mogollon cultures as far back as 200 A.D., in the Hohokam and Fremont cultures as early as 500 A.D., and more recently in the Navajo-Apache cultures as soon as the mid-seventeenth century. But his influence stretches much further than the peoples mentioned above. Even today in South America, medicine men roam the Andes mountains from village to village with flutes and sacks of corn on their backs. And in Tonga, the radio stations start each day by broadcasting flute music.

From his first millennium, Kokopelli was a medicine man, trader, and shaman, roving from place to place preaching peace and harmony, and teaching agriculture. Somewhere around the turn of the millennium, he became a fertility symbol and his likeness took on more than a hint of obscenity. He was said to be a rain priest and trickster. Maybe there are really several characters over the centuries who have merged into one.

The setting of this novel is the Apache culture in the mid-seventeenth century. Kokopelli is portrayed as one of the Three Nephites, or one of the three great shamans that had power over death. Every effort is made to accurately capture the flavor of such time and place.

Eye-to-Eye with the Bobcat

Eye-to-eye the bobcat and I studied each other. The cat seemed to be looking into my soul as I peered into hers, and what I saw I didn't like. Unless I missed my guess, the cat wasn't about to give way for the likes of me: a skinny *Tinneh* (Apache) boy that had wandered into the cat's domain.

My name is White Thunder, named that because a white thunderbolt danced around me on one occasion in my seventh autumn. I am a son of Meatas, who proudly wears the headdress of an Apache scout. Our village is a tiny one, as Apache villages go, having only one or two-hundred lodges. This moon we are located two days run north of the Gila River.

2—WHITE THUNDER & KOKOPELLI

The female cat hissed at me, still showing no signs of giving in. Some days cats can be cranky and unmoving. Of course a boy that has only seen twelve summers is not large enough to be very scary to the cat, at least I wasn't. I clutched a wooden spear in my hands, the tip hardened in the fire and sharpened to a fine point. I wasn't frightened, but I can't say that I was relaxed either. In an all out scrap with my cat sister, both the cat and I would lose.

Taking a couple of backward steps, I thought that possibly I could slip away. The cat advanced, matching my backward progress step for step. The situation didn't look good…maybe I would have to charge. Grandfather said that there isn't a member of the four legged tribes that won't give a little when a man charges with a stick. Yet giving a little ground and clearing out of my way are two different things.

Once again I peered through the cat's eyes, trying to search her soul and envision a communication of peace, the way Grandfather had taught me. Only through envisioning can you speak with the animal tribe, and they with you—spirit to spirit communication. We Apaches are the most powerful of all tribes. We call ourselves *Dinneh*, *Tinneh*, or *Inde*, meaning "the people," but only live people communicate with words. Even the ghosts that walk the earth in darkness, and Ysun, the greatest deity of all, communicates through thought envisioning, the same way that man communicates with the animal tribes.

For a brief moment I thought I saw hesitation in the cat's soul. Then my mind flashed to thoughts of a litter of kittens, probably in a nearby den, and the cat's determination was back. Her center of mass seemed to lower, and I saw that she was poised, ready to spring.

I surely wasn't prepared for a tussle with a cat. Dressed in the usual Apache skins, I wore high-topped moccasins that came almost to my knees, a soft leather clout, and a red cloth around my forehead that held my shiny black hair in place and provided a tie to anchor three colorful pheasant feathers. I wished they were eagle feathers, but I haven't earned eagle feathers, yet. It would be nice to have a layer of leather clothes to protect my skin from the cat's cruel claws.

I gripped my wooden spear, aiming it at the cat's center of mass. She hissed, sending a ripple through her powerful muscles. Not any larger than a small dog, the cat should have turned her bobbed tail and darted out of my way, or at least allowed me to back off, but now she would die—I refused to think otherwise. I closed my mind to the scratches I knew would come and prepared to impel the wary cat on the end of my spear.

The air smelled of rotting aspen leaves and forest peat, but in my nostrils the hot smell of battle was already gathering. I was vaguely aware of a bead of sweat slithering down my cheek to drip off the end of my chin.

A restless breeze rustled the leaves and lifted a lock of the cat's hair. As if Wind Maker was teasing the cat, a leaf floated down and landed on the cat's nose. She flipped it away with a sharp, irritated quiver of her whiskers. Wind Maker laughed at her, as only the wind can, then sang to the cat, moaning its death chant. Gradually Wind Maker's chant took on the quality of a reed flute.

A flute? Everyone knows that wind blowing through the trees doesn't sound like a flute. Yet it was a flute.

I shook my head, trying to clear it. It doesn't pay to get distracted over the sound of the wind when you are looking death in the eye. Tightening my grip on my wooden spear, I studied my foe. Maybe not as ready to pounce as she had been, she was staring into space or maybe looking beyond me. It's an old trick with men, but would animals know that trick? I wanted to glance over my shoulder to see what captured the cat's attention, but dared not. I could still hear the mellow strains of a flute floating on the breeze.

Again the cat's muscles rippled as she raised from her crouch. *What was going on here? Was the cat having second thoughts?* Something was wrong...not terribly wrong, just strangely out of place.

Taking a chance, I glanced over my shoulder, then looked back again.

Nothing.

The sound of the flute floated away with the breeze as a lone leaf fluttered to the carpet of decaying leaves on the forest floor. Returning my gaze to the cat, I noticed that her ears were erect, listening intensely to the deadly stillness. Even the insects had stopped buzzing.

Suddenly, giving me only a passing glance, the cat wheeled her graceful body and glided into the undergrowth. But before she disappeared, she cast me a final glance and bobbed her stubby tail. Then she melted into the shadows. From somewhere up ahead a faint chorus of tiny meows greeted the mother cat as she moved away from me.

Backing up, lest the bobcat have second thoughts about coming at me when my back was turned, I retreated until I felt safe. As I followed the music on the wind I saw, seated on a rock, a man with a flute.

Kokopelli!

He sat there, relaxed, as if he had been there all day. Of course I knew he hadn't because I had just passed the rock before I met the bobcat.

Kokopelli is a shaman who plays a flute as he goes from village to village spreading peace and harmony and teaching the art of growing melons, pumpkins, beans and corn. For the most part, everyone agrees that he is out of touch with reality, but he is a nice old man to have around, and he plays the flute beautifully.

No one knows how old Kokopelli is, which in itself is strange. He appears to have sixty or seventy summers, but they say he doesn't age. The old men in the village say he was an old man of sixty or seventy summers when they were children.

"You are Kokopelli, are you not?"

"You know my name. Have you seen me before?"

"I saw you only once from across the village, but everyone speaks of you. They say you are a great shaman."

"I do the work of Ysun (God) and Quetzalcoatl (Christ), nothing more. Of myself I am nothing."

"You spoke to the bobcat with your flute. She liked your music and it calmed her soul."

"The bobcat would have killed you, and it is not time for you to die. You have a mission to accomplish on this earth."

I bristled a little. "I am not afraid. Maybe I would have killed the cat."

"In a few years when you have gained a little more stature you would have killed the cat, but if you had a little more stature the cat would have been more willing to back away."

Realizing the great shaman was right, I studied him for a few moments. "When I passed this way a few moments ago, I didn't see you," I said.

"I wasn't here. I came when the cat called."

I caught my breath at his words. "You can understand the words of cats?"

"White Thunder, Ysun made all creatures and placed them on Earth Woman for the use of man. He takes notice when even a sparrow falls to the ground, so why should he not take notice of a mother bobcat and a young warrior?"

It made sense, but I didn't know that Ysun was a "he." I

didn't know what Ysun was, except for the force that created all things.

The chatter of the insect tribe snapped my thoughts away from Kokopelli, and I turned to listen. Again the wind whistled through the trees, no longer sounding like a flute, but sounding like the wind ought to sound.

Out of the corner of my eye I caught movement, and turned my head in time to see a wood rat dart to a hole. Brother Owl must not be around, else the rat wouldn't have made his move across the open.

Turning back to Kokopelli, he had slipped away. I hadn't seen him go. There was movement by a chokecherry bush. *Maybe he had gone there, but why?* More or less out of habit, I searched for his tracks and followed them as far as the chokecherry bush, where they disappeared. I wasn't surprised.

Turning on my heels, I was careful as I moved through the forest, as I didn't want to meet the cat's mate. It was almost time to meet up with Grandfather, and I had a ways to go.

• • •

The old man with wrinkled skin and keen eyes was seated in a water birch thicket at the edge of a small stream. Deer had made a bed in the edge of the thicket, just the right size for Grandfather. Yet it offered a view of the valley that I must cross in returning to him.

I had been with grandfather for five summers, since I was seven. When boys of my tribe reach seven summers, they are assigned a grandfather as a teacher. Fathers don't teach their sons because the fathers are needed as hunters, scouts or warriors, so grandfathers are the teachers. Some grandfathers have several students, but my grandfather has only one student—me—and he is my father's father.

As I jogged up, Grandfather didn't move, except for the smile across his face and the movement of his eyes. He waited for me to come to him. When I reached him, he motioned for me to be seated and handed me a handful of freshly-picked salmon berries. "Eat, Grandson, then tell me about the bob-tailed cat."

"H-how do your know about the bobcat?" I asked.

"The same way that Kokopelli knew."

"How did Kokopelli know? How did you know about Kokopelli?"

"Ask the owl."

It was the response Grandfather always gave me when he wanted me to figure out something for myself. The original meaning of the statement was, "Ask the owl how he knows when the mouse is going to dart for his hole," but it got applied to anything an adult wanted a student to figure out for himself. Clearly Grandfather hadn't spent the whole afternoon in the water birch thicket, else he wouldn't have known about the bobcat.

I told Grandfather of my experience and he interrupted now and again for clarification, as he always does. When I was completed, he began with, "Why did you stalk the bobcat, Grandson?"

"She is the cat whose hind paw leaves slightly larger tracks than the front paw. I wanted to see what she looked like."

"Did you see?"

"I saw, but all she wanted to show me was the size of her teeth and the volume of her snarl. But I almost touched her, Grandfather."

"You do well at stalking, White Thunder. You move as the wind moves, with a flowing motion that makes you hard to observe in the background of the forest, and generally you understand nature's silent language. But today you forgot to listen to the owl."

"Listen to the owl? I didn't see an owl."

"That's just it, Grandson. The owl wasn't there because hunting wasn't so good, and hunting wasn't good for the owl because the cat had frightened away much of her food. She frightened it away by repeated hunting for her young, which meant that her young were near."

I thought about what Grandfather had said. I had seen a wood rat, but the rat darted to its den when the cat's back was turned and didn't seem to be concerned with Brother Owl. Still, Grandfather seemed pleased with my stalking.

"Grandfather, isn't it time that I began training to become a scout?" It takes ten years of training to become a scout, under the guidance of the village grandfathers. During that time one lives alone and does one's own cooking. But I like being alone; I like my own company.

"I know you want to, Grandson, but the council won't discuss it until you have a vision telling you that a scout is your life's mission."

"But I have had many vision-seeking quests, Grandfather, and no vision comes. Soon I will be too old to learn the ways of a scout. I want to be like you and Father."

"You must appreciate, Grandson, that when you attempt to communicate with the World of Spirits, your spirit must be pure."

"How do I know if my spirit is pure?"

"Go to the stream and look at yourself. The Spirit-That-Moves-In-All-Things also moves in the streams and if you concentrate with a pure spirit, your image will begin to clear."

"I have done that, Grandfather, and once my image cleared as if I were looking into a pond. Still I received no vision to become a scout."

"Maybe, Grandson, you want to become a scout for personal gain, that you might feel more important in the village."

"It could be, Grandfather. I don't know where personal improvement ends and personal gain starts."

Grandfather stared at the trees, lost in thought. When his words came, they came slowly. "I am just beginning to learn that myself, Grandson. Keep in mind that you can't fight nature. You have to move with it. Likewise, you can't fight the will of the gods. You have to move with them."

I knew that as well as Grandfather, but still I was frustrated.

"I followed the footprints of Kokopelli after he calmed the bobcat with his flute," I said, trying to change the subject. "You know where they led, don't you, Grandfather?"

"I suppose I do. They led into the undergrowth for a few feet, then vanished."

"That's right. How does he do it, Grandfather?"

"I don't know, but if I were you I would listen to every word he says. He is a great shaman."

Bark of a Coyote

The evening breeze carried the sharp bark of a coyote. Starting with the usual yip, the bark ended in a coyote wail that gave off a slight echo. I froze in my steps, every fiber of my body strained to hear something—anything—because when a coyote howl echoes, it is man-made.

Nearly a year had passed since my encounter with the female bobcat, a year packed with Grandfather's style of training, which mimicked the training a scout might receive. Grandfather trained because he loved being a trainer. We would watch a track, returning to it repeatedly every little while for two or three days to see how long it took it to deteriorate. He was training me in all the skills of a scout, tracker and stalker. Fact is, he taught me to follow tracks at a run, the way Apache scouts do. Scouts can run all day from sunrise to sunset at an easy lope, following tracks.

Then one afternoon, after spending six days in the desert living on plants and licking the dew from rocks and leaves for moisture, I was on my way back to Grandfather, weak yet anxious to tell him what I had learned. I had been loping along before the coyote barked, but there I stood, holding my breath so that I could catch the slightest sound. When I didn't hear any more human sound, I prepared to slide into the undergrowth of the high desert browse. I slid my wooden spear in first to check the area for rattlesnakes, as I respect the rattlesnake's right to privacy. Nearby were catchaw and cholla cacti, so I was especially mindful to watch for thorns.

Apaches can hide anywhere, as the ability to track and hide is part of our heritage. But mostly we hide on our bellies, hugging Earth Woman. It's the fastest way to hide, and also the least likely way to be found, except by another Apache.

I had only a short time to wait until I heard a scuffle as if a wrestling match were taking place. Then human voices rose in the evening air. The words were Apache and were giving instruction to each other about holding something down.

Suddenly the scream of a deer shattered the evening air, telling the ghastly story. The hunters had captured a deer alive and were holding the animal down while they cut steaks from the live deer's flank. Some people say the meat is more tender that way.

It's a brutal way to slaughter an animal, though no more cruel than the wolf tribe does. Yet the grandfathers in our village have been following Kokopelli's teachings that man should be above the animal tribe when slaughtering game. And when you kill an animal, you should thank the animal for the sacrifice of his body that you might live.

There is only one family in our village that does not kill mercifully, politely thanking the slain animal for his body. They are Shi-Be and his sons, Sieber and Nan-Ted. Sieber is my age. He sort of holds to the teaching of the village grandfathers, but he has to live with his father just the same. It wouldn't surprise me a bit if it were Shi-Be and his sons butchering the animal.

Sieber's grandfather took ill during the winter and is walking in the Land of Shadows. But Sieber is old enough that he doesn't need a grandfather, so he spends much of his time with his father. "Grandfather" is a word that means "teacher," and much of the time they have no relationship to the students they are teaching. When a man becomes elderly, he either becomes a grandfather or goes off to die alone, as there is no place in a village for a useless man. Sieber and his father do things that Sieber's former grandfather would never have approved of, were he still living.

Slipping out from the desert undergrowth, I eased into a position where I could see the hunters. As I had guessed, I saw Shi-Be and his sons. The deer was still kicking, in the throes of dying.

I could have gone down and visited with the hunters, as they were from my village. But Grandfather had taught me that what they were doing was offensive to The-Spirit-That-Moves-In-All-Things and was against our village code of conduct. So I had no desire to meet them in those circumstances.

If you want to become invisible to humans in the forest or in higher vegetation, Grandfather says you need to keep your profile below chest level. So as I circled to higher ground, I ran bent-over, zigzagging through the cholla and desert deer browse. The sound of the screaming deer haunted me as I ran. There is nothing like spending a period of time in survival to make you feel that awareness of another living thing's needs is the doorway to The Spirit-That-Moves-In-All-Things.

As I cleared the ridge, putting a slow mountain between the hunters and myself, I straightened to my full height and ran with the wind. But my speed only lasted as long as my mind was haunted by the deer scream. My body had been badly used in my survival ordeal and soon I was barely plodding along.

Meeting Grandfather at our appointed meeting place, he sang me a "welcome home" chant as I jogged up. A grass mat was awaiting me, a sign that he was paying me a great honor for completing my ordeal.

I seated myself and he passed me a large container of water, watching me closely. I am sure that he was watching to see if I would gulp down large quantities of the life-giving liquid, or take only short drinks, the way he had taught me. I took short sips and he looked pleased.

"You were disturbed over Shi-Be and his son, were you not, Grandson?" he asked.

"H-how did you know?"

"Ask the Owl," he replied.

"How do you know what is going on, Grandfather? You don't appear to have moved from this spot."

"I have moved, Grandson. Tell me of your ordeal."

For hours we talked, and after a while Grandfather handed me some berries and dried meat. We then continued talking. Grandfather was a good listener.

As the sun settled in the west, Grandfather and I held our separate evening devotionals. Sunrise and sunset are set aside in our tribe for personal prayer. Prayer is an envisioning experience, so it can only be said individually.

At first I was envisioning a communication with The-Spirit-That-Moves-In-All-Things, then suddenly I realized that I was thinking of the screaming deer. The-Spirit-That-Moves-In-All-Things was communicating with me. I had the eerie feeling that the incident was going to play a major role in my future, yet how could that be?

• • •

The false dawn graced the east when I awakened the next morning and cast my gaze around for Grandfather. He was gone, but that didn't surprise me. Grandfather and Kokopelli are much alike in the way they both seem to come and go with the shadows.

As I prepared for my morning devotional, I noticed the sticks placed a certain way in the peculiar stick writing. As far as I know, stick writing is something that only we Apaches have developed. All it said was, "Well done, Scout."

Happy, I created a personal sweat lodge and cleaned myself up because you don't want to go home after an ordeal looking as if you had just been through an ordeal. You want to appear strong and brave as all Apache men do. Then I started for our village.

The Hoot of an Owl

There are things a young warrior never forgets, especially if he has reached the ripe old age of thirteen summers, as have I. He never forgets that he is to be a hunter, warrior, scout, or whatever, but the lodge is for the womenfolk. Even medicine men have to be hunters or food gatherers of some type while they are perfecting their trade, else they starve. And even medicine women have to care for a lodge.

As I approached the lodge, it was clear that Nantan Lupin (Gray Wolf) had been there, courting my sister Laughing Grass. In front of the wickiup was a pony. Ponies are generally for women because Apache warriors seldom use them, at least not to the extent that other tribes use them, according to the stories grandfathers tell. Apache men are starting to ride horses, but generally they are runners. Some of the scouts run sixty or seventy miles in a day, whereas a horse will lather up and die if you run him that far. And when you are mounted on a horse, it is difficult to quickly disappear into the undergrowth should an enemy appear. So Apache warriors generally eat the horses the women don't want. Women, on the other hand, use horses when they move the village, as they do often.

So the pony standing in front of the lodge obviously had to be for Laughing Grass as a marriage proposal, at least that is the way it seemed to me. If Laughing Grass fed the horse or took it water, that meant that she accepted the proposal. Knowing my sister as I do, she might play hard-to-get by waiting a day before she fed and watered the animal. If the pony was still unfed and watered at the end of four days, Gray Wolf could do nothing but collect his almost-starved horse and go his way, probably to dine on horse steaks as he licked his wounds.

As I approached the lodge, Grandmother stood in the entrance, studying the two large rats that I clutched in my hand. She looked pleased.

"You did well, White Thunder," she said. "Your meat will make a good addition to the evening meal." I grinned, liking the way that Grandmother always found something positive to say about everything I did. I handed her the rats. Once a hunter reaches the lodge with the meat, his job is finished.

"Go fetch some wood," she directed. "Laughing Grass is walking among the trees, communing with White Painted Woman." White Painted Woman is another name for Earth Woman or Mother Earth. I scowled because gathering wood was a woman's job. Besides, I had just been through a major ordeal and the family didn't seem to even want to know about it. It just wasn't fair. But when Grandmother said to get the wood, you got the wood—regardless. Besides, I could understand why Laughing Grass might have other things on her mind besides fixing the evening meal.

Hoping that no one would see me doing women's work, I made my way to the most likely place to find deadfall. As I gathered, I felt eyes following me. Trying to act casual, I didn't immediately look up. When at last I gathered courage and glanced up, I wasn't faced with a taunting peer, but I was gazing into the sparkling black eyes of Towhee, a girl my age.

Dressed in the traditional Apache style of the day for women, Towhee's dress was made out of two deer hides, finely tanned, made almost white with the lye from the campfire ashes, and sewn down each side. When it was new, the dress had been decorated with porcupine quills, but buckskin lasts a whole lot longer than quills, and the quills had mostly broken or fallen off. The moccasins she wore were very similar to mine, high-topped and good protection against low cacti. She cast me a curious smile, and I wondered about it.

Towhee used to be obnoxious, but in recent years my opinion of her has changed. As a child she was named Chubby Toes—now there's a name for you. But as she grew up she was named after the brown towhee bird, and the name was shortened to Towhee.

"Laughing Grass is away from the wickiup, wandering in the forest as she considers marriage with Gray Wolf, so someone has to do the women's work," I blurted out. "Besides, I don't mind it." The part about not minding it was more self talk than my true feelings.

"I will help you," she said as she started gathering sticks. Suddenly I really didn't mind doing women's work. If in the company of Towhee, most any task I undertook took on a new meaning. Strange I should feel that way.

Wood gathered, we made our way back to the lodge, each with an armload of firewood. Seeing Towhee and I together, Grandmother eyed us curiously, her mouth slightly turned up at the corners, but she said nothing. We dropped our loads by the wickiup, and I would have liked Towhee to have lingered longer, but she didn't.

Grandmother already had a fire going in front of her lodge and quickly added some of the firewood Towhee and I had brought. No sooner was it ready than Mama brought out an earthen pot of water and put it in the coals. When the water was boiling, Mama dropped the rats into the water, one by one, by their tails.

Rats are cooked as they are brought home—no cleaning or skinning, you just plop them into the boiling water and let them boil until done. When cooked they are fished out and left to cool a few minutes. To eat them, you pull aside the hide, exposing the tender tidbits of meat. Then you pick off the good meat, stuff it into your mouth, and throw away what remains.

The usual mealtime chatter was gone and we ate mostly in silence, each wrapped in his or her own thoughts. No doubt Mother and Grandmother were thinking of Laughing Grass and her potential marriage. Father was gone because Grandmother was in the lodge. In Apache culture, it is polite for the husband to leave the lodge when his mother-in-law enters so that she can have a good visit with her daughter. And when a mother-in-law enters, the husband is not to look at her directly, out of respect. So when Grandmother enters our lodge, father leaves and unless it is inclement weather, he doesn't return until she is gone.

Occasionally a groom will marry a girl and her mother, if her mother happens to be a widow. That way he doesn't have to pay respect to her as a mother-in-law. In the Apache culture, polygamy is accepted.

Apache culture is matriarchal. When a man marries, he leaves his mother and father's lodge and no longer has responsibility to hunt for them. His bride builds a new lodge for them by her mother's lodge and his responsibility as a hunter is redirected to the wife's family. Sometimes mothers will try not to become too close to male children because they know that when the boys get married they will be lost. "Raise a girl and you have her for life," the saying goes. "But if you raise a boy, you have him until he finds a wife."

Suddenly, as if feeling guilty, Grandmother broke the silence. "Where have you been all week, Grandson?" The job of a grandmother is to drill the grandchildren, particularly the grandchildren less than seven years old, each night on everything they have seen or heard during the day. If you have seen a bird, she wants to know what kind of bird, the color, size, and mannerisms. Sometimes grandfathers get involved too, though they are mostly interested in the student assigned to them. After you have rehearsed everything you saw or did during the day, then the teaching begins: names of animals are supplied, as are mannerisms and other interesting things. All animals are divided into four tribes: those that walk on all fours, those that swim with fins, those that creep or crawl, and those that fly. Insects are just insects, a pest from some evil force.

I probably should have told grandmother about my ordeal, but I seriously wondered if what I did would impress her. The grand news of Laughing Grass's proposal seemed to be on everyone's mind.

I don't know why I did it, but I found myself blurting out, "Yesterday I saw Shi-Be and his sons, Sieber and Nan-Ted, just after they butchered a deer. I heard the deer scream."

"You heard the deer scream? Isn't that unusual?"

"When I got to a place where I could see Shi-Be and his sons, they were holding the deer down, cutting steaks from its flank while it was still alive."

"That is not good," Grandmother said, displeasure showing on her face. "Kokopelli teaches that it displeases Earth Woman and The-Spirit-That-Moves-In-All-Things to treat the four-legged tribes cruelly."

• • •

The evening meal was over and I was walking past the council lodge where many of the grandfathers and warriors were in deep conversation, when I was waylaid by Shi-Be. "Well, there is the liar now!"

Caught off guard, I froze in my tracks. Shi-Be was facing me down with darn near all the men in the village watching.

"I don't understand," I said.

"You told the village that my sons and I cut steaks from a deer while it was still alive!"

"I didn't tell that to the village. I told it to Grandmother."

"See," Shi-Be said, turning to the men, "he admits it's a lie!"

"I just said that I told it to Grandmother, not to the village. But it is true that you cut steaks from a deer while it was still alive."

"Then you lie!" Shi-Be bellowed. "I and my two sons all say that you lie, and I will kill you for it." He drew his knife and started for me.

Someone pushed me out of the way and I fell, scrawling in the dirt. When I glanced over to see what had happened, I saw that Father had pushed me aside and was facing Shi-Be, both men holding flint knifes.

"We'll have none of that!" Beyotas spoke up. Beyotas was

the village Peace Chief and the ranking clan leader.

"But the boy lied!" Shi-Be insisted.

"I hear you," Beyotas replied. "Three to one you have determined that the boy lied. The men of our village have stopped butchering animals in that cruel fashion. But he is just a boy and he will not be killed!"

"I am not a liar!" I insisted. "I saw what I saw with my own eyes!"

"Go!" Beyotas snapped, turning to me.

• • •

News spread quickly through the village. Back at Mother's wickiup I sat in silence, pouting.

"I am not a liar," I said to Grandmother. "But why did you tell the grandfathers of the incident?"

"I don't know why I told the grandfathers," Grandmother admitted. "It just seemed like the right thing to do at the time."

Leaving the wickiup, I made my way to a ridge near the village and sat there looking at the stars that were barely coming out. Only when Towhee seated herself beside me did I know of her presence.

"You walk as quietly as a boy," I said.

"Quieter than most boys," she corrected me. "I'm just out collecting firewood so I must be back soon. But I saw you up here on the hill and wanted to come to you."

"Are you sure you want to be with a person that the village has branded as a liar?"

"The villages haven't all branded you as a liar, White Thunder—maybe some have, but not all. But it wasn't something that Beyotas wanted Shi-Be and your father getting into a knife fight over."

We sat in silence for a few moments, enjoying each other's

company. I knew she had to get back with an armload of firewood, so she couldn't stay, but I was glad she came.

"Come help me gather firewood, White Thunder, so I won't be away from the wickiup too long."

I nodded and rose to my feet, and together we gathered firewood. I would have gone clear back to her mother's lodge with her but she declined, saying, "I will return alone. I don't know how Mother feels about you this evening." So I left her the firewood and returned to my seat on the ridge.

Down in the little valley directly below me, someone had kindled a fire, and I watched the red and orange sparkle. Thoughtfully I considered the worlds of fire, breath, water and the current world. To understand us Apaches, you need to understand the four worlds, because they are represented in a lot of what we do. We Tinneh people believe that we are living in the fourth of four worlds, the first being the world of Fire. A burning mass was flipped from the sun and it became the earth. That mass is represented by the color red and it's direction is east. So we love the color red and turn our faces east in the mornings to meet the rising sun.

The second world is Breath, and the process of breathing is sort of a prayer in itself. It is represented by the color blue, and its direction is South. The third world is Water. It is represented by the color yellow and its direction is West. And the fourth is the world in which we now live. It is represented by the color white and it's direction is North. When we came to the current world from the underworld, we came through holes in the earth, represented by the hoop dance. Red, yellow, blue and white, the colors of the world, make up all other colors. And the directions comprise four of the six directions, the other two being down to Earth Mother and up to Father Sky.

Lost in thought, I glanced up as someone else was climbing

the ridge. Studying the approaching person, I saw that it was the shaman, Kokopelli. I would have liked to have seen Grandfather, but he apparently hadn't returned to the village. But Kokopelli was almost as good.

"Keep seated," he said as I started to rise. He took a seat beside me, pulled out a flute, and for a while played beautiful flute music.

"What is it that you play, Kokopelli? It sounds like a love chant."

"It's not a love chant," he grinned. "It called Moroni's Chant, and was composed by a righteous man that was all alone." As Kokopelli continued to play, I glanced down at the village and could see villagers casting glances our direction. Only after a long time of playing did he put the flute away and begin to talk.

"You have learned a hard lesson," Kokopelli said, looking directly at me.

"You mean that you think that I am a liar, too?" I asked.

"I know that you are not a liar this time, White Thunder, but there are times in your life when you have lied. There are times when all mortal men tell lies."

"I don't understand what you are getting at, Kokopelli."

"I am trying to tell you to never be ashamed of telling the truth. You never, never have to lie."

"I didn't lie about Shi-Be and his sons butchering the deer, but there are times when everyone has to lie or else they will hurt someone's feeling over something or other."

"White Thunder," he said, looking me squarely in the eye, "you never have to lie. You may have to say you don't wish to talk about it, but you never have to lie."

It's odd how Kokopelli looked me directly in the eyes, the same as I looked into the eyes of the bobcat. In my culture you look at people's mouth when they are talking to you, not at their eyes. You only look at their eyes when you are studying their soul, as I was with the bobcat."

"What about those in the village who think I lied?"

"You just let them talk. All over the country people say false stories about me. They even draw false picture writings, picturing me as a fertility symbol and an evil man. They even say evil things about Quetzalcoatl."

"Quetzalcoatl, the feathered serpent?"

"Yes. Quetzalcoatl represents the only perfect man that ever lived, and people accused him of being a liar. So I guess that if people tell lies about Quetzalcoatl and me, you will just have to assume that they will tell lies about you also. The important thing, White Thunder, is to never lie."

"W-who are you, Kokopelli, and how do you know so much?"

"Who I am is not important, White Thunder. It is what I can teach you and the other villagers that is important." He slid out his flute and once again started playing Moroni's Chant. Then he arose, bid me farewell, and departed as quickly as he arrived.

• • •

Making my way back to the village, I went to Mother's lodge, trying to avoid people. Mother and Father were there, speaking to each other in hushed tones as I seated myself in my usual spot. I pulled a skin robe around me, forming a rocking chair, and started rocking.

"I heard flute music coming from up on the side of the mountain," Father said, "and I thought I saw you up there with Kokopelli, and before that Towhee was with you. The two of them are about as good of friends as a man can have."

"Your eyes see clearly, Father. Kokopelli said that people

sometimes call him a liar, the same as Shi-Be and his sons called me a liar."

Father just grunted. Father never was much of a talker. For a time everyone sat in silence, each lost in his or her own thoughts.

Suddenly the quietness of the evening was broken by the hoot of an owl.

As if shot from a bow, Father's back snapped straight and the color drained from his face. I glanced at Mama and she seemed as white as I imagined White Painted Woman would be.

The hoot of an owl near the lodge meant death!

To avoid the death foretold by the owl, our village would be moving in the morning.

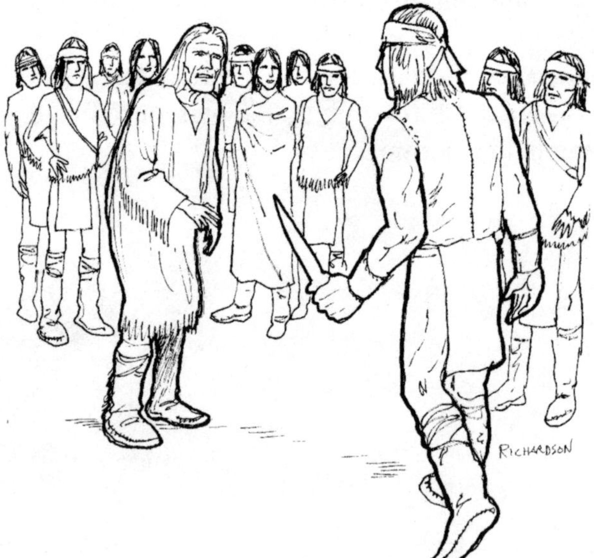
RICHARDSON

The Heat of the Day

The heat of the day had not yet set in when we moved out the next morning. As usual, the women and children took down the lodges, packed everything, and carried the loads. The men stood guard or went hunting so that when we stopped for the night there would be meat. But the men didn't want me with them because I had been labeled a liar the night before. So my job was to help the women move.

I helped take down the lodges and pack. Then, when we moved, my job was to lead Laughing Grass's pack horse. Yes, Laughing Grass made a quick decision to marry Nantan Lupin when it was moving time and the pony was available to use in moving.

Nantan Lupin was no where around, as you might guess. His task, the next task in the marriage proposal process, was to provide Laughing Grass with some meat he had killed, so he was out hunting. Then after he brought it in, it was Laughing Grass's turn to show off her cooking skills—alone—without the slightest intervention from Mama and Grandmother.

On all sides of us the warriors had fanned out to protect the village because when a village moves, it is vulnerable. Powdery dust rose in small billows, coating everything with fine powder and advertising our location for miles around.

I glanced behind. Towhee was immediately behind me, her usually shiny black hair coated with powdery dust. I had an idea: as long as I had to do women's work, I might as well walk beside Towhee, provided, of course, that her mother wasn't against me and would allow me to walk beside her daughter.

Glancing both directions to see who might be watching, I slowed my pace and moved to one side. Towhee soon moved up beside me. On her back was a cradle board with her sister's papoose. The little tyke glanced at me and gooed softly.

"You getting tired, White Thunder, or did you just want to drop back and walk with me?" Towhee asked. She surely had a way of getting my intentions out in the open, quickly.

"This here pack pony whispered into my ear that she wanted to fall back and walk with you. Naturally I had to fall back too, as I come with the pony." I quickly glanced over at Butterfly Catcher, Towhee's mother, to see if her face showed any displeasure at my walking beside Towhee. Her face showed nothing.

"I see you are considerate of the four-legged tribes," Towhee said with a mischievous grin, something quite typical of her.

"Actually I like the two legged tribes too...at least the ones that goo at me from under the shade of a cradle board." I would have liked to have said something flattering about the girl that carried the cradle board, but my shyness, coupled with a little uncertainty, prevented it. So we walked on in silence, a silence broken only by the commotion over a smoke signal to our right.

"What does it say?" Towhee asked.

I cast her a wondering sidewise glance. I didn't know that girls couldn't read the dots and dashes of the smoke signals as well as us boys. After all, Grandmother and Mama seem to be able to read the signals. Smoke writing is something unique to us Apaches; other tribes, such as the Navajos or Zunis, don't use smoke or stick writing.

"It says that the scout found a body. It is the body of a white man and he has been scalped."

"A white man? I've never seen a white man, though I have heard of them."

"You have seen Kokopelli. He is white, at least whiter than the rest of us, though his eyes are the same color."

Towhee stiffened and her face showed the expression of horror. "Do you think it is Kokopelli's body they found?"

"No. Rumors have it that he can't be killed, and if it was Kokopelli, they would have said so. The smoke writing says that he is a black robe."

"A black robe?"

"Yes, a priest of the people who conquered the cannibals."

"You mean the Spanish?"

"Yes, the Spanish. The scalped man is a Spanish priest. They wear black robes. They are very powerful people or else they couldn't have defeated the cannibals."

"The cannibals are called the Aztecs," Towhee set me straight.

The Aztecs used to raid the country to the north and take

prisoners alive. Then they would sacrifice the prisoners to Huitzilopochtli, the sun god, then bury the heads and give the bodies to the masses for food. Our Apache ancestors discouraged the Aztecs by making an example of all the Aztecs they found. The favorite method was to hang the Aztec prisoners upside down over a low fire, then have the women and children skin the prisoners alive. But the Aztecs have been conquered for generations, and we Apaches still torture our prisoners the same way. Kokopelli says that such practices should cease.

"Our people generally don't scalp," Towhee said, breaking into my thoughts.

I nodded. She was right. Scalping was more of a plains Indians practice, though occasionally the Spanish will scalp.

"Likely someone other than an Apache did it," I muttered the obvious. Conversation died out, and we walked on in silence, except for the papoose on Towhee's back, which was in a gooing mood.

• • •

Suddenly he was there. Kokopelli. No one seemed to notice his approach, not even the scouts assigned to keep us safe.

Addressing himself to Chief Beyotas, Kokopelli announced, "You will need to change your course and flee for the mountain retreats."

"Why?" Beyotas asked.

"The Spanish soldiers are on their way to punish your village for killing the black robe."

"We didn't kill him. You have taught our village to be a peace-loving village and to call all men *salmann* (friend)."

"Yes, I know that you didn't kill the priest. You have followed my teachings well. But if you are going to live long enough for me to teach you further, you will have to make a new home among the hanging valleys of the higher mountains. Do as I say and you will be safe."

"You are a great shaman and well respected. We old men believe your words because we know that you speak with a straight tongue, but our young men do not always follow us. They will not believe you."

"I, for one, do not believe you, Kokopelli!" a voice broke in. All eyes turned toward Shi-Be. Where he came from, I surely don't know. I thought he would be with the warriors guarding the column of women and children. Shi-Be seemed to want to be where the action was, not where the work was.

Kokopelli appraised Shi-Be for long moments, moments that made the warrior uneasy. Then, as if dismissing Shi-Be as an unruly upstart that didn't deserve his further attention, Kokopelli returned his gaze to Beyotas with instruction. "Do as I say, Beyotas. Most of the men will follow. Those that do not follow will fight the Spanish and either die or be taken slaves to the Spanish mines many days' travel to the south."

"How dare you come in here and try to take over this village, Kokopelli?" Shi-Be shouted. "You are not even of our village and are not actually our shaman. It's about time someone stood up to you and put you in your place!" He drew his flint knife from his belt and advanced toward Kokopelli. It seemed that Shi-Be was always drawing his knife and threatening someone.

Standing where I was, I had a frontline view. Kokopelli was on my right and Shi-Be was on my left. Silently, I slid the reins of Laughing Grass's pack pony into Towhee's clenched fist. Kokopelli was unarmed, and I wasn't about to stand by and see one of the few friends I had killed by the likes of Shi-Be.

I had to hand it to Kokopelli, he sure didn't appear scared. Fact is, he appeared rather bored with Shi-Be, which was a surprise to me because Shi-Be is a dangerous man—about the best fighter in the village. And, as I said, Kokopelli was unarmed, without a prayer against Shi-Be.

Abruptly a grandfather offered Kokopelli a knife so that he wouldn't be unarmed. But to my surprise, he declined it. Kokopelli was going to die, and he wasn't even going to protect himself!

I glanced at Shi-Be, seeing his lips parted in an evil smile, and suddenly something snapped within me. Even if it cost me my life, I was going to do something about it!

As Shi-Be passed my position, I stuck out my foot, hooked Shi-Be's ankle with my toe, and pulled.

He went sprawling in the dirt!

Surprised, but springing back up like a cat, he turned his attention to me. "If it isn't the liar! Well now, I'll just make short work of you! You're nothing but a coyote!"

There are no curse words in the Apache language. When you want to curse at a person, you call him a coyote or a bug or something repulsive. To be a coyote is bad, which isn't to be confused with being a coyote teacher. A coyote teacher is a grandfather that teaches in a particular style. He teaches the way a coyote kills an elk: one nip at a time.

"I'm not a liar, and you know it, Shi-Be. You're a liar and you browbeat your boys into standing behind you in your lies. Even if you kill me, you'll still be a liar!"

Shi-Be was close now, and there were no warriors in the column to stand beside me. None of the grandfathers were young enough for a knife fight with Shi-Be.

I was going to die!

Shi-Be's knife flashed, and so did mine. I would die, but I would go down fighting. Shi-Be's knife missed, but he missed on purpose. He was just testing me before he sank his knife into my heart. There was a streak of red on his thrusting arm—guess my knife didn't miss. At least I drew a little blood.

We were circling now, the experienced fighter and me. Then it came, the thrust that would take my life. But I wasn't there, I had jumped back, and Shi-Be was laying on the ground. What was wrong? Why was he down there, not moving?

The villagers gathered around. Gaping. Wondering.

The crowd parted and Kokopelli made his way to the inner circle and ordered everyone back. He knelt down beside Shi-Be and rolled the warrior onto his back.

"Shi-Be," Kokopelli said softly, but loud enough for all to hear, "do you hear me?"

Shi-Be nodded.

"Your left arm and face are paralyzed, but I think you can walk a little, if you try. See if you can walk."

Shi-Be tried to speak, but couldn't. Then he gathered his feet under him, and with the help of Kokopelli, rose to his feet. He stood there shaking, but he was standing.

The clan leaders looked at each other, but nothing was said until Beyotas verbalized their unspoken decision. " We will go to the mountain valleys as Kokopelli directs."

Kokopelli said nothing, but took the reins of Laughing Grass's pony from Towhee and handed them to Shi-Be with the words, "You have two good legs and one good arm, Shi-Be. You will gain your strength in a few days. I am sure that the village needs White Thunder as a scout, and since all villagers have to be useful, you can lead the pack horse for him."

Then turning to Towhee and me, for Towhee was then standing beside me, Kokopelli said softly, "To be willing to give your life for a friend is the greatest of all loves. White Thunder, you will never die in combat as long as you never lie."

Then, touching me gently on the head and Towhee gently on the arm, he slipped through the crowd.

I glanced at Towhee and we exchanged wondering glances. We returned our gaze to Kokopelli but he was gone. That's so like Kokopelli: he arrives and departs so suddenly that no one knows how he does it.

• • •

I served as a scout and messenger for the village as they trekked on toward the mountains. Most of the young warriors and their families stayed with us. But some of the young men went out to fight the Spanish and never returned. We don't know what happened to them but we suppose that they are either dead or slaving in the Spanish mines.

Lean and Mean

We had left the village for a day of stalking the elusive bobcat—Towhee, Bylas and me. Bylas is Towhee's brother, a lad with ten summers. He is quick to learn, fun to be around, and good company for Towhee and me.

Grandfather had not returned to the village after my six days in the desert. Everyone was worried about him, but no one knew anything. Without Grandfather I had no trainer, but even with Grandfather I was generally alone. Our new home where Kokopelli lead us was not far from where the female bobcat had held me at bay until Kokopelli calmed the cat with his flute music. I had told Towhee about the cat and she immediately started pressing me to take her to see the cat firsthand. Apparently Towhee had never seen a live bobcat, so her curiosity was richer than her common sense.

The bobcat stood aloof, lean and proud atop the boulder. At the base of the boulder, half hidden in the delicate bluebell flowers and green foliage, three half-grown kittens romped. But the mother cat's eyes were not for her kittens, though her protective instincts were. Her eyes were for Towhee, Bylas and me, crouched across the narrow, deep canyon behind a thimbleberry bush.

"She's beautiful—so soft and cuddly," Towhee said, almost breathlessly as we watched the cat family.

"She may be beautiful and proud, but she doesn't look cuddly to me," I replied.

"Not the mother cat," Towhee corrected. "The kittens playing with the other cat's tail."

"Oh. Well, she does look soft and cuddly," I granted, "but I don't know if it is a she or he."

"She is studying our every move!"

"She is? She seems to be contentedly playing with the other kitten's tail."

"Not the kitten; the mother cat, silly."

"Oh. Yes, she is watching us, but I think we are quite safe because it's a long way to the bottom of the canyon and back up to us, and she won't want to leave her kittens exposed."

"She's gone now. The den must be close to the boulder."

"She doesn't look gone to me, sitting up there big as life."

"Not the mother, the kitten."

"Yes, the kittens are gone. Shall we go to investigate?"

"No, silly. At times you're an awful tease, White Thunder."

"Yes, but sometimes I'm just confused. What were we talking about, anyway?"

"You wanted to go."

"Yes, but not just yet. Right now I want to study the cats,

but on the way home there are some things that I want you to see."

"What is it?"

"Picture writings on the rock wall that talk about Kokopelli."

"How do you know they are about Kokopelli?"

"They were made by the old ones who used to live in this land when the Aztecs roamed the land south."

"Then how could the picture writing refer to Kokopelli? He isn't that old."

"I can't answer that, Towhee, but the pictures are there, large as life. We'll see them on the way home. And they talk about Kokopelli as if he were alive hundreds of years ago. Fact is, the picture writing talks about three men like Kokopelli. They are all the same, all playing a flute."

We watched the cat family for hours, studying their ways. Of course Towhee and I enjoyed each other's company also, and we didn't mind Bylas, who was content to let Towhee and I do all the talking.

Apaches are taught to study every aspect of an animal. You need to know how an animal protects himself, how he hunts, what foods he likes best, and what his tracks look like both when he is leisurely walking, and when he is stalking. It is not unusual for an Apache boy to spend all day watching an animal's tracks or to return repeatedly throughout the day to see at what point the soil falls in on the track, or how long it takes for the grass to spring back. We Apaches consider ourselves good stalkers and trackers, but it takes a lot of time and patience.

As the sun moved across the sky, the three of us knew we had to be getting back. The decision made, we made our final appraisal of the graceful mother and her litter of three, then slipped away as silently as three shadows. It amazed me that Towhee walked every bit as silently as Bylas and me.

• • •

On the way home we routed ourselves by the picture writings I had told Towhee about, the ones that pictured Kokopelli. It was the first time I had seen Towhee so surprised; she just stood there for a few minutes in awe.

"They are ancient writings," she muttered after a while of examining them, "yet they picture Kokopelli."

"Yes, but look at this, Towhee." I showed her some more petrography that contained three Kokopellies.

"You mean there are three men like Kokopelli?" she said. It was more of a statement than a question, as she continued reading what the picture writings seemed to say. All three Kokopellies were hunched over, playing a flute. The hunch signified an old man of forty years or more, and the flute represented peace and harmony.

"There must be three men," I acknowledged, "but the grandfathers of the village only speak of one." She nodded. She, too, had only heard of one Kokopelli.

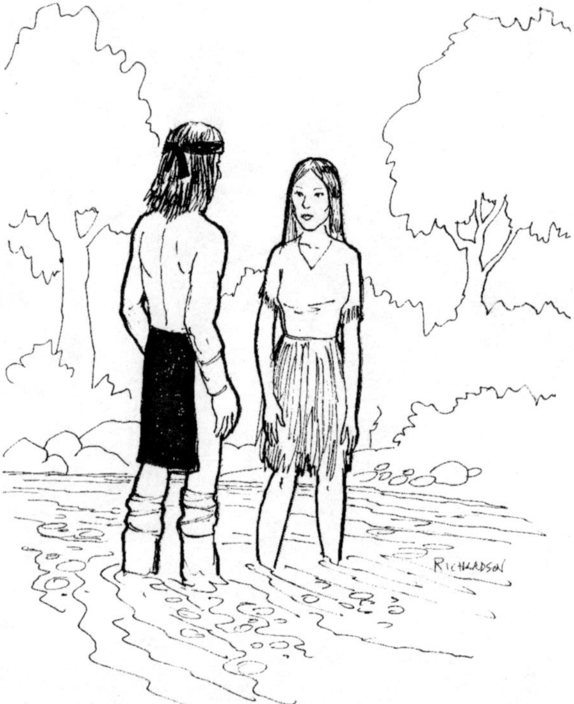
RICHARDSON

Eyes as Bright as a Squirrel's Eyes

Her eyes were as bright as a squirrel's eyes as Towhee studied me from across the tiny stream. Then her gaze rested on two plump rabbits and a crude, hastily-constructed basket.

"What's in the basket?"

"Mesquite beans," I replied.

"You seldom come home empty-handed, White Thunder."

I could feel the color gathering in my face and saw the gleeful twinkle in Towhee's eyes as she started teasing me.

"You'll make some woman a fine warrior some day, White Thunder. I'll have to remember that at the next squaw dance. It'll cost you plenty to win your freedom."

Squaw dances are girls choice, and are particularly fun for

all. When a single girl catches a boy, he dances with her until he buys his freedom by giving her something of value, such as a pretty stone, feather, claw or a piece of cloth. The boy mainly dances in one spot while the girl holds onto the back of his belt and dances in a counter-sun-wise circle backwards. And he has to dance in that one circle where he can hardly even see the girl, until, as I said, he buys his freedom.

Though it is polite to only look at a person's mouth when they talk—not their eyes—I could not help but see both. Towhee's mouth was turned up at the corners, and she was having a great time. People particularly look beautiful when they smile.

"Maybe I won't want to buy my freedom, Towhee. Maybe I'd prefer dancing with you until I get so dizzy I can't stand up."

"It's a sign of weakness to get dizzy, White Thunder. You don't want to let me see you showing weakness, do you?"

"You have me there, Towhee," I grinned.

She returned a beautiful smile, so characteristic of her, then bent to the stream to fill her water jug. Her jug was a clay pot as large as a very large melon. On one end it was flat so that it could stand up, and the other tapered to a narrow neck, then flared out again into a bell. Around the neck of the jug, a head strap was anchored. With the jug full, she swung it to her back, positioned the head strap in the center of her forehead, then let her head accept the weight of the jug.

Dropping her hands to her side, Towhee stood there as if she had something more to say. A gentle breeze caught her long silky black hair and rustled the grass of her colorful grass skirt. During the summertime the maidens of our village like to make their clothes out of bear grass and other plant fibers. Though rough material, the girls say that they are cooler than doeskin dresses, but best of all, they accept bright plant dyes, the brighter the better. Around her neck and across her chest and waist Towhee wore several strings of berry and bone beads. Unlike the Navajos, who also call themselves "The People", we Apaches do not make much silver and turquoise jewelry. Our women favor the pretty things of the earth.

Towhee, herself, is one of the truly pretty things of nature, I thought as she just stood there studying me as if she had something more to say. I shook my head to clear it and glanced down at the stream. A fish swam past. There are tribes that eat fish, but not ours—not unless it is a matter of starvation. When Giver of Life (Ysun) made the fish tribe, he didn't intend them as food for the Apaches.

Gradually I became aware that Towhee was speaking and glanced up.

"You didn't hear a word I said," she accused as I gave her a blank stare.

"I guess I didn't," I admitted.

She beckoned for me to cross the stream, so I did. Once across, she slid close to me and spoke in hushed tones.

"Shi-Be has been drinking strong *tulapai*, made by his woman the way he likes it—*strong*. Under the influence of the drink, he told Sieber that he is going to kill Meatas."

"Father?"

"Not so loud, White Thunder."

"Why would he kill Father?"

"Not just your father; he also says he is going to kill Kokopelli."

"But why?"

"You know as well as I do that you and Kokopelli made him look foolish when we were moving from our desert home."

"Then why not kill me and Kokopelli rather than Father and Kokopelli."

Towhee shrugged. "I don't know, but..." she offered, hesitating a little and examining my expression, possibly to see if I would take offense.

"But what?"

"But you are not a proven warrior, and I suppose that he considers it no great feat to kill you."

I guess my face clouded a little. Just how long does it take someone to grow up anyway? I have spent all my life and I still haven't proved myself as a warrior. *At least,* I thought as I studied Towhee's eyes, *she had the tact to call me a warrior rather than a boy.*

It had been almost a year since we moved to the hanging mountain valleys. Shi-Be's arm had returned to normal just as Kokopelli had said it would. But everything was not as they had been before; there was no longer open fear from the villagers when he spoke—maybe there never would be again. Often you would see him up in the rocks alone, brooding.

"Shi-Be may try to kill Father," I muttered, "but I doubt that Kokopelli can be killed. Where is Kokopelli, anyway? I haven't seen him for moons!"

Putting her hand gently on my shoulder, Towhee turned to me so that I was looking directly at her. Her eyes were sincere, her voice soft and her words were carefully chosen.

"I do not worry about Kokopelli," she said as I studied her lips. "I worry about your father and you."

Faces Painted Red

The mountain yarrow was in full bloom as the messenger beat his way through the pass and loped down the ridge, through the pines, and into the village. His approach was announced by a gossiping magpie, the noisiest bird in the mountains. Face drawn in the throes of distress, it was clear to everyone that he carried unpleasant news.

"Meatas is dead, killed and scalped!" he announced.

My heart froze in my throat as my mind clouded first with disbelief, then with horror. The villagers were pressing the messenger for details and I mutely listened to their questions and the messenger's response with stunned silence.

The awful wailing of the death chant snapped me back to

reality, such as it was. The wailer was Mother, now a widow.

"Shi-Be," I whispered. Deep in my intestines I knew that Shi-Be was responsible. It made no difference that Father's corpse was scalped, something Apaches seldom do. Shi-Be could have scalped him in an effort to hide his guilt. Oh, he'd have some type of an excuse, of course he would. You just didn't kill another villager, especially in secret. If there is a just cause for fights to the death, it would be witnessed by the tribe. If you kill in secret, it is called witchcraft. Murder, grave robbing, calling on the evil spirits, it's all witchcraft in the Apache culture. It's punishable by death, too, but only if proven.

A hand on my shoulder drew my attention and I glanced into the comforting eyes of my brother-in-law, Nantan Lupin. "Don't be too quick to judge, and don't do anything rash," he said. "You don't know that he did it."

"I don't know that who did it?" I asked, studying his lips.

"Shi-Be," he replied. "I saw you glance at his wickiup, and I know what I would be thinking were I in your shoes."

"Do you also know that he threatened to kill both Father and Kokopelli?"

"No, I didn't know that, but I'm not surprised. Yet threatening to kill someone and doing it are two different things. And even if he did kill your father, if you pick a fight with Shi-Be he'll kill you.

Nantan Lupin's words were almost drowned out by the sounds of a second then third mourner. The second was Laughing Grass, and I don't know who the third was.

I wished for Grandfather, someone to talk with. *Where was Grandfather anyway? Was he walking in the Land of Shadows?* No one seemed to know, but we all suspected he had met his death somehow.

∴

My people are nervous about taking care of the dead, even when "the shell" belongs to a loved one. We are not afraid of dying, just timid at anything that has to do with the dead. We handle the body as little as possible. Then those that care for the body purify themselves before returning to their former duties.

Those sent to attend to Father's body wore only clouts and painted their faces red with red ochre mixed with tallow. In a crowd of villagers, yet strangely alone, Mother had the look of a little old grandmother. We were all with her: Laughing Grass, Nantan Lupin, and myself. Most of the village followed yet Mother seemed to have eyes for none of us, only for her warrior, who was no more.

When Father's body was prepared, the attendants carried it to a crevice and lowered it down. With Father's shell was placed many of his possessions, along with a little food and corn for making *tulapai*. Then, to the mournful strains of the Apache death chant, the crevice was filled with rocks, and some sacred corn pollen was sprinkled over the top. The attendants left the burial site walking backwards and leaving confusing footprints.

As we trudged back to the village, the *makah* (medicine man) slipped something into my hand, but no words were spoken. Glancing down, I saw that it was Father's flint knife. Generally a warrior's knife is to be broken when its owner dies. In giving me Father's knife, the *makah* was giving me the instruction that it was my duty to avenge Father's death with the knife before I broke it. Casting my gaze around to see if anyone had seen the *makah* give me the knife, I saw Kokopelli watching intently, his forehead wrinkled and mouth drawn slightly in a frown.

"Where did he come from?" I must have asked aloud.

The *makah*, walking beside me, glanced in the direction I had indicated. "It's the first time I have seen Kokopelli in moons," he replied. "I didn't see him at the burial."

• • •

We mourned for four days, as the spirit remains for four days before it leaves for the Land of Shadows. Father's possessions that had not been buried with him were burned, save for his flint knife.

Shi-Be was mourning with the rest of us, an act that confused me, as he clearly didn't care for Father. Maybe he wasn't Father's murderer, I thought, yet his mourning plainly lacked sincerity.

On the fourth day I was sitting among the rocks as Kokopelli approached and seated himself beside me.

"Haven't seen you since the day Father was killed," I said as he approached. "I was hoping you would come around. Please sit with me and talk."

"What would you like to talk about, White Thunder?"

"I have a feeling that you already know, Kokopelli. You seem to know all things."

"You want to know why I appeared displeased when you were given your father's knife to avenge his death."

"Uh-huh," I replied in awe, but not surprised that he read my mind. Apache shamans read people's minds often, using the principle of envisioning.

"Vengeance belongs to Ysun, the Giver of Life, White Thunder. He is in charge of all things."

"He?" I replied. "I didn't know that Ysun was a he."

"Yes. Regardless of your tradition, White Thunder, Ysun is a male person, and he reserves vengeance for himself."

"But Father would be displeased and degraded if I failed to avenge the dead."

"White Thunder, the dead don't need to be avenged by you. Ysun will take care of that."

"But I don't want Father to wander the shadows, unavenged. Where is Father anyway? Is he in the underworld, the clouds, or the shadows?"

"He is in the World of Spirits here on the earth, working out his own salvation with Ysun. The exact location is unimportant to you, but your father is an honorable man."

"Is?"

"Yes. He is very much alive in the World of Spirits."

"What about Mother? She is all alone and needs the comfort of knowing that Father's death was avenged."

"I worry about her because she refuses to be comforted. You need to take care of her and sustain her as best you can. If need be, your father will have to come back from the World of Spirits and speak with her, but for now she is mourning so much that she wouldn't accept him."

"You seem to know much, Kokopelli. Do you know what happened to Grandfather? We haven't seen him around."

"Your grandfather is in the World of Spirits also. He and your father are together."

"How do you know that?"

"How I know is not important, White Thunder, but I know. He had perfected himself very highly and is now being taught the ways of Quetzalcoatl. You must work hard if you wish to be like him."

"I want to be like him, but of course I wanted to become a Scout also. But the vision didn't come and I couldn't get a council meeting from the grandfathers."

"Your grandfather taught you the skills of a scout, but your mission on earth is not to become one. Ysun has another mission for you."

"Isn't it about time that Ysun let me know what my mission is? All my friends are well along in their training and I still am not a proven warrior."

"We must not take it upon ourselves to instruct Ysun or The-Spirit-That-Moves-In-All-Things, White Thunder. Did not your grandfather counsel you to have a pure spirit that could be counseled?"

"Yes, he did," I said timidly. "He told me to allow my inner vision to grow within me until it filled my soul."

"Then follow his counsel, White Thunder. Allow your inner vision to grow and also allow The-Spirit-That-Moves-In-All-Things to teach you. Until then, make yourself the best village hunter or warrior you can. Just do whatever is needed in the village."

I studied the ground, knowing Kokopelli was right. He sounded much like Grandfather and Father.

We talked for a while longer, then Kokopelli excused himself and disappeared over the saddle of the mountain. I was left to think long and hard about his words.

• • •

After the period of mourning, loneliness seemed to set in for Mother, a loneliness she could not shake. She burned the wickiup and built a new one that Father had never slept in, but still couldn't remove the loneliness. She would hang on to me for long moments before I went hunting or left for the day, telling me to be careful and watch out for coyotes. Some of the older generation held to the notion that the evil spirit rode on a coyote across the face of Earth Woman when the long shadows of the evening merged with the stillness of the night. It's not that coyotes are evil animals, it's just that they are mischievous and frequent the burial crevices of the dead.

Then one day when I returned from the hunt, Mother wasn't to be found. Sensing something was wrong, I left the meat I had killed at the entrance to the lodge and went in search of her, watching for her footprints. Apache scouts can tell the footprints of everyone in our village, so I knew Mother's footprints when I saw them.

Her footprints led to the cliffs. My fears mounted that she had gone out alone to die. The older generation of Apaches seem to have power over life and death. They can die by just willing themselves to die. Maybe even Grandfather had willed himself to die, yet if he knew he was going to wander off and die, surely he would have told me.

The quiet of the mountain was disturbed only by the relentless drumming of a mountain woodpecker. It was a steady drumming as if the woodpecker had been at it a long time.

As I approached the cliffs, a marmot whistled the alarm and Mother looked up from a perch high on the cliffs where she sat, leaning against a scrawny foxtail pine. It was a spot with a good view that she went to often, and had even constructed a frame on which she placed pine boughs for shade on hot days. Turning my feet her direction, I made my way to her.

"Why do you follow me, White Thunder?" she asked. Her words surprised me because, though accusing, they carried an air of peace. In the past few weeks Mother had not displayed much peace, only ceaseless mourning.

"I was worried about you, Mother."

"Worried? Why?"

"You are my mother."

"Maybe I haven't been good company," she said. "I just came out here today to view the beauty of Earth Woman."

For as long as it takes the sun to move one hand in the

western sky, we sat in silence. Apaches are a patient people, and can sit in silence for hours.

"There is a kill back at your wickiup, Mother," I said, feeling the pull of hunger within me.

"Your father visited me today," she replied, ignoring my reference to food.

I just stood there with mouth open, studying her lips, then her eyes.

"You have spoken with Father's spirit?"

"Yes. He came to tell me not to mourn his death any longer."

I grinned. "Kokopelli said that he might."

"Kokopelli?"

"Yes. About the fourth day of mourning Kokopelli talked with me as I sat up in the rocks. He was worried because you were mourning too much, and he said that Father might visit you from the World of Spirits and tell you not to mourn so much."

"Kokopelli is a great shaman with great wisdom if he told you that. What else did he tell you?"

"He told me that Grandfather was also in the World of Spirits, his name for the Land of Shadows. And," I added hesitatingly, "he said not to avenge Father's death."

Mother frowned. "Your father's death must be avenged, else he will be dishonored."

"I know that, Mother, and I told that to Kokopelli. But Kokopelli still insisted that Ysun doesn't need men to avenge the dead."

"His words are strange, White Thunder. I know he is a great shaman, but someone needs to avenge your father's death."

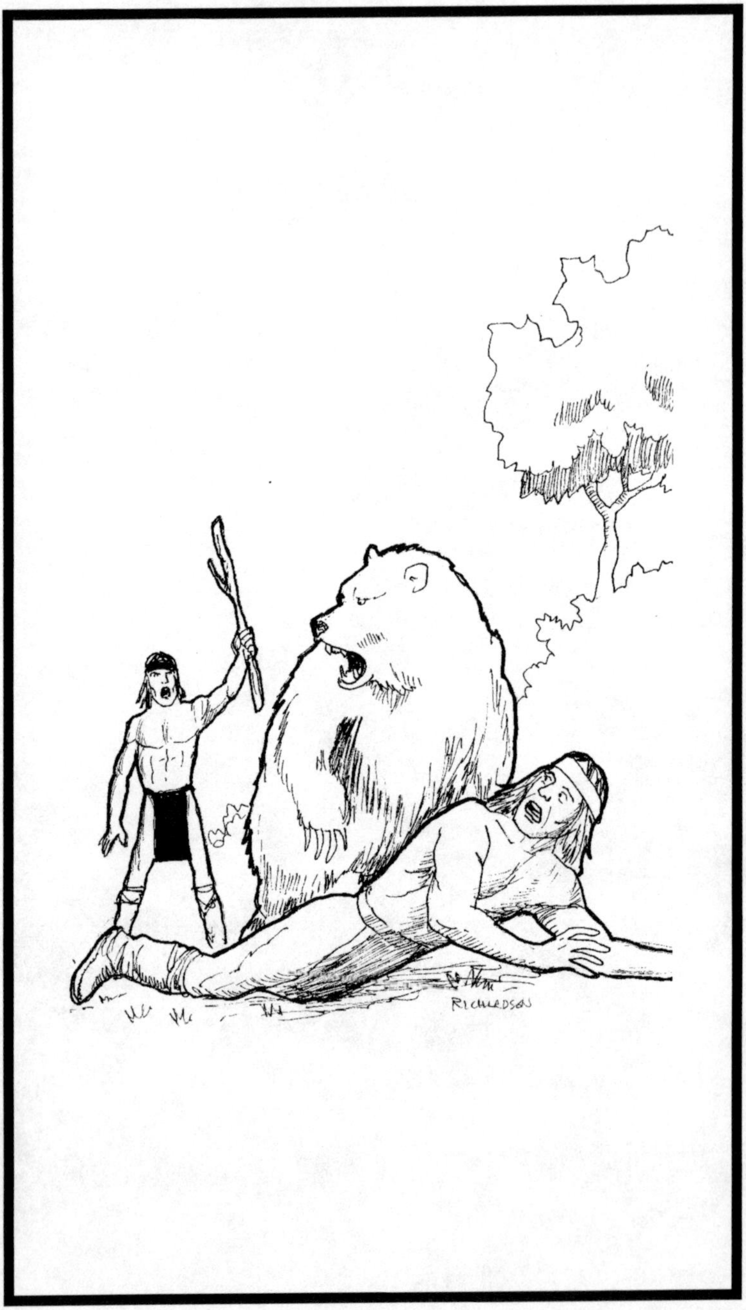
RICHARDSON

Medicine Feathers

A year had passed since the death of Father and I had fifteen summers. No longer a boy, my muscles were solid and my eyesight keen, at least to my way of thinking. Of course, I wasn't always the last to remain on my feet in an all-out Apache wrestling match, for which I had Sieber to blame. Thick necked and strong as a bear, Sieber was the only one that I seldom beat, though I could always beat him in a foot race.

Good friends in spite of my apprehension of his father, Sieber and I did many things together. We became warriors together and often hunted with each other.

A five-striped chipmunk was twitching his striped nose at

us from under a buckbrush bush the morning Sieber and I decided to get some medicine feathers, the soft downy feathers that come from the eagle. It was a bald eagle we were after, though we would accept the offerings of a golden eagle if he chose to take our bait.

Except for an occasional pillow cloud, the sky was clear and the hunting seemed good for the feather tribe's birds of prey. So with high hopes, Sieber and I set out to prepare our trap and collect our reward.

We located a natural crevice in the boulders and tossed in large enough rubble to lodge a few feet down, creating a platform for us to stand on. Over the top of the crevice we placed pine boughs, then went in search of a rabbit for bait.

Sieber, who announced that he would take first turn at catching the eagle, also said that he was going to use live bait so that the squeal of the rabbit would attract the eagle.

"Can't you imitate a rabbit squeal good enough to fool an eagle?" I questioned.

"You can never imitate the squeal of a rabbit and make it sound exactly like the real thing," he replied, an air of finalization to his voice. I shrugged and followed him to a likely spot for catching a rabbit.

Ever try to run down a rabbit? I can run one down, and have done it many times, but Sieber has a little more weight to him than I. He is built more for pushing down a tree than chasing a fleeing rabbit.

Lying under a chokecherry bush near a rabbit run, Sieber and I established our blend with the mountainside and waited, breathing with the breeze. All went well until a yellow jacket decided to make an extensive exploration of Sieber. I'll have to hand it to the yellow jacket, he was a persistent little beast, but was beginning to bring out the cranky side of Sieber's nature.

Apache warriors practice snatching flies to give them agility. If you can snatch a fly, surely you can snatch a harmless little white tailed bunny as he passes within grabbing distance. But when brother bunny came hopping down the rabbit trail, Sieber had just about reached his boiling point with the yellow jacket. Still, Sieber saw the hopper and, ignoring the yellow jacket, made his attempt for the rabbit.

When you snatch a fly or a rabbit, you're not supposed to move your whole body, just your arm. But in his irritated state, Sieber moved his whole self, advertising his intent to the little hopper, and missed the critter completely. But not about to be beat by a rabbit, he leaped to his feet, the chokecherry bush tearing at his bare skin, and dashed after the white-tailed critter. After all, it was the only rabbit that had passed us all morning. And I'll have to hand it to Sieber, he was giving that little bunny a run for it.

Up the rise and through the brush, Sieber was determined to catch that little rabbit before it got to its hole. I couldn't even see Sieber but I could hear him. By the noise he was making, he was anything but a stately Apache warrior. I began to chuckle as I realized what the telling of his chase would sound like after I spiced it up and told it around the campfire come evening.

Suddenly the crashing through the underbrush took on a more serious sound. I realized that Sieber was returning, running as if the rabbit had miraculously gained stature and was chasing him. When he burst into the opening, he was running as though he had seen a spirit, leaping rocks and crashing through bushes. When he saw me, he tilted back his ample neck and bellowed, "*Chuska* (bear)!" He had only made a dozen more strides when a brownish-colored black bear came crashing through the underbrush, tearing into the open behind Sieber.

Right off I knew that Sieber was in trouble, because a fast runner he wasn't, even when being chased by a bear. To make matters worse, as he tried to leap a mountain mahogany bush, his feet snagged on the fuzzy seed trails and he went down hard. The bear, a female that was apparently nursing, let out a roar of delight that told me that Sieber was a dead man unless I did something and did it fast!

Roaring as if I were a bear myself, I grabbed a stick and charged the bear. As far as I know, there isn't a four-legged animal alive that won't initially give in when charged by a man with a stick. So initially the bear gave ground and backed up, turning her attention to me rather than to Sieber. Assuming that Sieber had enough sense to hightail it out of there while the going was good, I kept the bear occupied.

After a few minutes the bear had completely forgotten about Sieber and charged me. But I pride myself on being able to run like an antelope, and Sieber had already winded the bear, so it was hardly a fair race. After less than a mile, the bear gave up and loped off, probably to find her cub.

Some time later, when I finally located Sieber he was trying hard not to sulk. "Cottontails are messengers of the Evil Spirit!" he snapped as he rested against a fir. The older generation often associate cottontails with the devil, or Evil Spirit, because they live in crevices where burials have been made. For such a large bear of a man, Sieber looked so much like a whipped puppy that all I could do was laugh. At first he took offense, but soon he was laughing along with me.

Our laughter relieved our tension, and soon we were back trying to catch a rabbit for bait. Only this time, when we saw one, Sieber dispatched the rabbit quickly with a wooden-tipped rabbit arrow.

• • •

Hidden, I nestled in the boulders and watched Sieber do his thing. Crouched in the crevice with the pine boughs across the top, Sieber had placed the dead rabbit on top of the boughs for bait. Sieber wiggled the bait while imitating the squeal of a wounded rabbit to attract the greatest of all birds: the eagle. If the eagle struck, it was Sieber's task to grab the eagle by the legs, just above the talons. The talons, of course, would be buried in the rabbit, and Sieber would quickly pull the eagle's bottom half down, into the pine boughs so that the bird couldn't use his beak. Then Sieber would pull out the feathers he wanted and turn the bird lose.

That was the plan, but to our surprise, a hawk, not an Eagle, took the bait. Sieber should have seen it was a hawk and pulled the bait through the boughs and let the bird pass, but he didn't see that it was a hawk soon enough. The bird struck, Sieber grabbed his legs, and to his disgust he was harvesting hawk, not eagle, feathers.

Oh, did I ever have a story to tell around the campfire!

• • •

Up the boulder-strewn mountainside, Sieber trudged to where I waited, his face clouded in disgust and disappointment.

"You're not going to tell about this around the campfire, White Thunder," he said. It was a threat, not a question. All I could do was laugh, and the more I laughed the more his poker mouth turned into a grin. He knew that I'd tell, and that the whole village would enjoy a good laugh at his expense.

"Well," he said, "let's go home."

"But Sieber," I stammered, "it's not time to go home! There

is still a lot of daylight, and besides, it's my turn to get some eagle feathers."

"They won't hunt this late in the day," he replied, though his voice lacked conviction. "Only hawks hunt this late in the day."

"Eagles hunt all the time...almost. And it is my turn!"

"All right," he replied, knowing that I was right. "We'll have to get another rabbit because the hawk took the one I had."

We went after a rabbit, hoping we could find one. Yet the mountains are teeming with rabbits, and by then we knew where their burrows were.

Moving with the wave of the grass, we closed in with bows ready and arrows fixed. It was an easy shot. The first rabbit that came bounding down the rabbit trail was mine. Sieber watched attentively as I politely thanked the rabbit for the use of his body, then gathered up my prize and lead the way to our eagle trap.

Inside the trap I waited, imitating the squeal of a hurt rabbit as I peered through the boughs for any signs of a bird of prey. It was hard to see through the boughs, and I gained appreciation for Sieber's inability to immediately detect the difference between an eagle and a hawk.

The sun moved two hands across the afternoon sky as I waited, and my imitation of a squealing rabbit took on an increasingly poorer quality. The pillow clouds gave way to high, thin clouds, and in the south it appeared as if a storm was gathering. Still I waited.

A marmot came over to investigate, opinionated about his neighborhood. From the ridge a gray fox examined the trap. He was clearly interested in the rabbit, but the breeze was blowing his direction, so maybe he caught my scent.

I was about to give up when I caught a glimpse of an eagle

circling. I couldn't tell if it was a bald eagle or a golden eagle, but clearly it was an eagle. Excitement mounted within me and I sharpened my imitation of a squealing rabbit.

You don't use any covering for your hands when you catch an eagle, it's all done bare-handed. If you miss and the eagle gets you with his beak, your hand sustains major damage, but seldom do warriors miss because once you grab the eagle legs, it is a natural instinct to pull your hand down. All you have to remember is to keep a hold of the eagle's legs.

The eagle dove and I knew he was going to strike. I knew it, I knew it, I knew it! In my mind I had already snatched the birds legs in my big hand before he struck, and was holding on for dear life to the legs of the mightiest bird in existence!

The eagle struck!

I grabbed and pulled the legs down into the boughs, and with my left hand I busily harvested selected feathers as the huge bird bounded me up and down with the sheer power of his thrust. I didn't even know if I harvested feathers from a bald eagle or a golden eagle nor did I have time to care.

Task completed, I let the bird go and my joy mounted into the crescendo of an Apache war cry. Sieber came down the slope and joined in my joy. Fact is, it surprised me that he took so much delight in my success.

Gathering up an assortment of bald eagle feathers, I turned to Sieber. "Now it's time to go home," I said.

Trekking home, we were two friends vowing that we would always be friends. His father had ceased to be antagonistic toward me and life looked good.

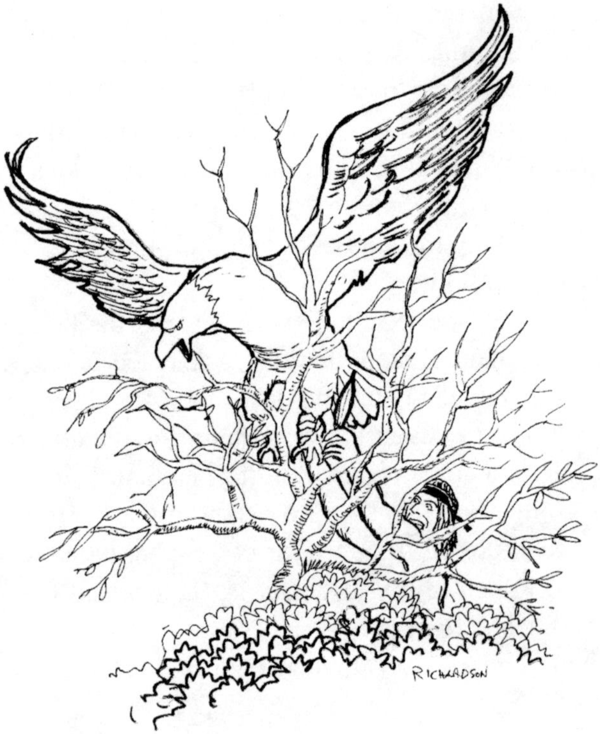
RICHARDSON

Cat Whiskers

The yellow brittlebush flowers were in full bloom as I made my way down the rocky slopes to the desert floor. The early autumn of the mountains made it a good time to go hunting at lower elevation, escaping the chill of the mountains.

Rounding a boulder, I was stopped still in my tracks by the sight of a large lizard munching on a prickly pear. The lizard, a chuckwalla, was as long as my forearm, and highly prized for food when my people lived near the desert.

Always on the lookout for food, the job of an Apache hunter, I quickly fit a sharp wooden-pointed arrow to my bowstring and prepared to harvest the meat. The chuckwalla swung his whole body around with one easy heave of his thick tail that he uses as a club for defense, and was facing me head-on.

My bowstring was half drawn when I caught movement out of the corner of my eye. Casting a sidewise glance to my left, I then forgot the chuckwalla as I eased off on the string and slid to my knees in the sandy soil, crawling under the gray-green leaves of a sacred datura plant. Seeds from closed flowers trickled down my neck. The sacred datura flowers close during the sunlight, but this time of year the seeds are being dropped. My mind was on the two strange men walking up the arroyo.

One of the two men bore Comanche features and the other man was thin and wiry. His face was dark with sunken cheeks and cat whiskers, like the Utes sometimes have. Yet he didn't have the hair style of a Ute nor did he have the round face. Fact is, his long, skinny face looked more like the Spanish yet he clearly had some Native American blood.

I laid there on my stomach, breathing only when the grasses waved. Whatever the reason for the men being in the arroyo, they were up to no good. Comanches were the ancient enemy of the Apache—the only tribe to ever beat us in battle.

They stopped at a large sacred datura plant, and the man that I had mentally nicknamed "Cat Whiskers" busied himself harvesting a palm full of seed. I cringed as he popped the seeds into his mouth. He must be sick, I thought, as sacred datura seeds are a pain reliever and narcotic.

The two men stood around as if waiting for someone. Cat Whiskers broke into a fit of coughing which ended as he spit up blood. The Comanche backed off as if he didn't want to be around the sick man. Making his way twenty paces to a boulder, he mounted it and looked around, clearly expecting someone.

As if appearing from nowhere, a muscular man with a stomach that was running to paunch emerged from behind a mes-

quite bush. I caught my breath and stared in disbelief.
Shi-Be!

Seating themselves in a circle, Cat Whiskers produced a pouch of something that appeared to be tobacco and filled a pipe. Offering the stem to the sky, the earth, and the four directions, the three men smoked as if they were the best of friends. Their conversation continued for an hour or more, but I was patient—curious too.

They talked in sign language, something Apaches seldom do. Comanches and the tribes to the north are big on sign language but Apaches have had little use for it. Still Shi-Be had to learn sign language somewhere. I wondered where.

Shi-Be smoothed out the sand at his feet and started drawing a map of some type. Then he pointed in the direction where our village used to be before Kokopelli moved us to the mountains. He started drawing again. Cat Whiskers seemed to be listening intently, but periodically they had to stop talking as Cat Whiskers broke into a fit of coughing.

Cat Whiskers reached into a pack he was carrying and pulled out a knife, the likes of which I had never seen before. It was shiny and the flint was smooth, if indeed it was made out of flint. I have heard of a substance of which the Spanish make knives that is as good or better than flint and doesn't break.

Extending the knife to Shi-Be with both hands, Cat Whiskers waited as the Apache almost reverently accepted and examined it, obviously pleased. Then Shi-Be bent to his map and made some final adjustment. It appeared that the knife was a bribe to get Shi-Be to finish the map. Then as Shi-Be reverently examined his knife, Cat Whiskers peered over the map, apparently committing it to memory.

Satisfied, Shi-Be blended back into the same mesquite bush where I had first seen him. Cat Whiskers and the Comanche turned on their heels and retraced their steps back down the arroyo.

Though it was highly unusual, there was nothing wrong with Shi-Be meeting with the strange companion, except maybe the Comanche. To give a Comanche anything more than a knife in his belly is considered treason by most Apaches. The only thing wrong that I could detect was an unholy feeling of evil that seemed to fill the air during the meeting. Something was very wrong!

I waited until the insects told me that everyone but me was gone, then gave it an additional wait for good measure before I moved. Being patient helps you to live long enough to become a grandfather. I looked for the chuckwalla, but it takes a very dumb lizard to wait around to become someone's meal.

It is the Apache way to not return by the exact route you came, unless there is clearly not another convenient route. So I made my way down a slope that was thick with hedgehog and pincushion cacti with an occasional ocotillo. Picking my way through, I headed for a stream that flowed intermittently from the mountains. Rich with tall sycamore trees and home to more desert critters than I cared to count, it was my stopping spot to replenish on water for my long trek home.

I swatted a pesky insect as I sidestepped an ugly but harmless hairy tarantula and made my way to the ribbon of a stream. Then I tanked up on water Apache style, gorging myself with water until I was more tick than Apache.

Storm clouds were gathering as I readied myself to travel. Low on the horizon lightening flashed. I moved out, but had only gone a short distance when a man stepped out from behind a sycamore.

Shi-Be!

I'll have to hand it to him, he knew his stuff. Quiet as a breath, even the insects didn't seem to take notice of his presence. He was everything that a good Apache warrior should be when it came to his stalking skills. He was standing there with a look of triumph in his face.

"You were following me!" Shi-Be accused.

"No. Not following you, but I saw you with the Comanche and the sunken cheek man," I replied. Maybe the tone of my voice carried a little more insolence in it than it should have.

"You saw nothing!" Shi-Be snapped. "You'll deny that you ever saw me if questioned!"

"I don't intend to lie for you, Shi-Be, and I don't know why you want me to. Why should the villagers care if you meet with the Comanche and the sunken cheek man with the cat whiskers. Are you doing something wrong?"

Apparently it was the wrong thing to say, as Shi-Be pulled his new knife from his belt and lowered himself into a slight crouch. The corners of his mouth turned up in a grin—not a nice grin. Shi-Be's knife seemed to be his answer to every problem; anytime he got angry he pulled his knife.

"You have mouthed off to me one too many times, White Thunder. You decide that either you saw nothing today or I'm going to kill you the same way I killed—" He caught himself before he said what he was going to say.

"The same way you killed who? My father?" I accused. "Did you kill Grandfather, too? Maybe because he found out that you cut steaks from the deer while the deer was still alive?" I was just talking. Fact is, I hadn't even guessed that Shi-Be might have had a hand in Grandfather's death until I started talking.

Shi-Be was taken back a little. It wasn't necessarily anything I said but I clearly wasn't acting afraid of him. Right there and then it appeared that he decided to either throw fear into me or kill me. It was hard to tell which.

"You're a dead coyote, White Thunder. I'm going to kill

you and I'm going to do it slowly, taking pleasure in making you retract your words before you die. The villagers will never know what happened to you!"

My mind flashed back to Kokopelli's words of nearly two years ago, the day I tripped Shi-Be when he was bent on taking Kokopelli's life. "You will never die in combat as long as you never lie," Kokopelli had said. Yet it looked as if I was going to die, and I was certain that I would rather die in combat with him than take his sadistic torture.

"Clearly, Shi-Be, you are the coyote. You're a coyote and a liar. And it doesn't matter whether you kill me or not, you're still a coyote and a liar, and you know it!" I was talking braver than I really was, as I wanted him mad enough to kill me rather than just wound me and torture me. Yet in the back of my mind I still had faith in Kokopelli's promise that I should not die in combat. I suspected that the promise encompassed all kinds of death associated with combat, even Shi-be's brand of torture, whatever it might be.

Shi-be's grin broadened. Oh he was enjoying it! He reminded me of the bobcat I had run across many years earlier, and I found myself looking into Shi-be's eyes, trying to search his soul as I did the bobcat's. Clearly something was bothering him.

"Don't look into eyes!" Shi-Be snapped. "It's taboo!"

As far as I know it's not taboo, it's just considered impolite. Of course, I don't know all of the taboos and myths of my people as I have not even reached my sixteenth summer. Legends are told during the summer and myths are told during the winter, and sometimes on certain moons in the winter. So if a boy is away from the lodge, sometimes he doesn't hear all the myths and taboos. Now girls, on the other hand, are always home so they are much more knowledgeable on Apache myths and taboos than boys. Still, I looked deep into

Shi-be's eyes and it was obvious I was making him uneasy.

"You trying to capture my soul!" he snapped. There is a belief that people who peer into other people's eyes are trying to capture their soul.

Suddenly I suspected what Shi-Be was up to. I had heard of the Spanish sending agents in search of the yellow metal that they prized so highly. Then when they found someone that would tell them where it was found, they moved in with their armies and created a mine, making the local Indians slaves.

Dry lightening flashed from the pending storm, which had not yet reached us. The lightening was not close, but it was bright.

"That's white thunder that you are seeing, Shi-Be. It is what I was named after."

"You're a witch!" Shi-Be screamed, and I realized that he was shaking and sweating. "You're a witch!"

"You aren't going to kill me, Shi-Be!" I said calmly. Within me I knew that no one would ever kill me in combat unless I told a lie. It's Kokopelli's promise.

"You're right! You're right!" he said, backing up. "I won't kill you! I'll tell the village that you are practicing witchcraft, and they will kill you!" Witchcraft is one of the few things punishable by death, though there are a lot of things that are categorized as witchcraft.

"Shi-Be," I said, "why don't you go home and think this thing through? While you're at it, figure out a way to explain your new Spanish knife to the villagers."

I guess he thought going home was a good idea, or at least he liked the idea of getting out while the getting was good, as he was already backing up.

I surely didn't know what I did to throw fear into him, but I had an idea that *I* hadn't done anything. It was all part of Kokopelli's promise.

• • •

Shi-Be slipped into the desert and I was again left alone. The storm seemed to have passed us on the east. Following the ribbon-sized stream, I made my way to high country with the intent of hunting along the way.

The sun was only two fingers above the western mountains when I killed a rabbit for my meal. Roasting the meat over a low fire, I felt the chill of the evening and the need for warmth. So I created a long, low fire to warm the ground. Then, when it appeared that the ground was warm, I scraped the ashes to one end and used them to warm my feet as I lay on the warm earth and slept.

As I slept, I dreamed of Grandfather. He was hunkered down over a cup of a fire, asleep. That was like Grandfather; he would build a cup of a fire and go to sleep on his haunches with the fire between his knees. Over his shoulder would be a blanket. I could never sleep that way because I kept falling over when I fell asleep, and I was afraid of landing in the fire. I would either heat the ground, build leaf huts, or just burrow in deep leaves to keep warm.

In my dream I wanted to awaken Grandfather to talk to him, but I didn't know how.

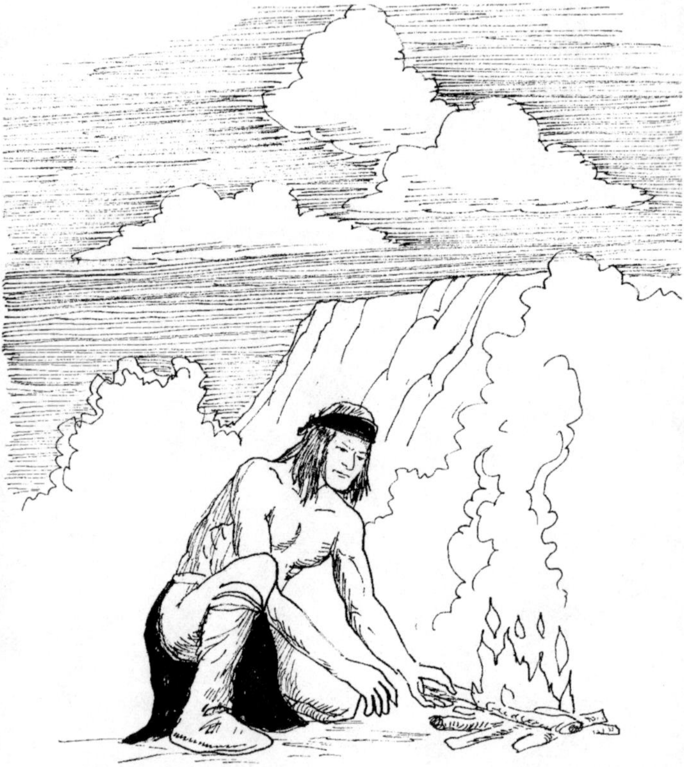
RICHARDSON

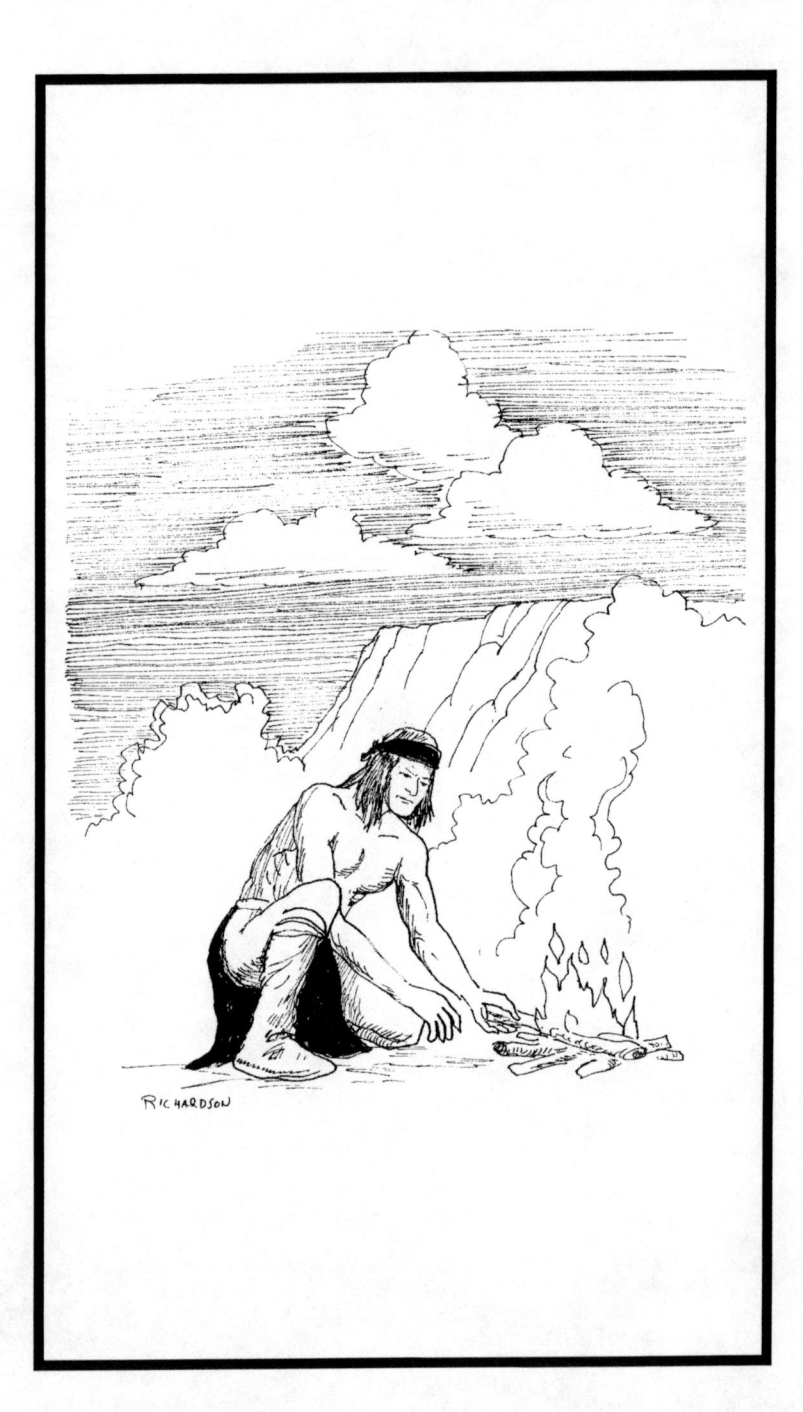

The Old Chant

I harvested a buffalo, a fine one. Buffalo meat is a real treat for our people, as they are scarce where we live. They didn't used to be scarce, but the meat was so popular that the buffaloes were over-hunted. Our buffaloes aren't nearly as large as the buffaloes on the plains, but they represent a lot of good meat.

Creating a travois, I loaded the buffalo and used myself as a pony. It was a hard pull, but we hunters are used to doing what it takes to get the meat home. I didn't have far to go and it was mostly downhill.

Crossing the only ridge on my way to the village, I heard the sounds of a chant. It was a catchy chant that I had never heard before, and I didn't know the words because it was sung in the old language. The Apache language changes over the generations in spite of all that we can do. Words change as well as the way we say them. In time the language changes. The shaman and the grandfathers know many of the words of the old language, but there are some that no one knows.

As I drew closer, I saw that the singer was an old woman. She stopped singing and observed me draw closer.

"That is a fine buffalo, White Thunder," she said. "There used to be many such buffaloes in these mountains, but they have mostly been hunted out."

Surprised that she knew my name, I was speechless. Pausing, I eyed her curiously. Dressed in the dress of a grandmother, she seemed strangely familiar.

"I probably should know you, Grandmother," I said, "but I don't."

"I am not important," the grandmother said. "Can you repeat the chant I am singing? It is not hard."

I sang the chant and she gave me a few corrections. Then together we sang it through a few times.

"What is the meaning of the chant?" I asked.

"It is a boyhood chant about a young man on his first hunt. But the exact meaning is not important. What is important is that you sing it as you enter the village. You know Eskiminzin, don't you?"

"Of course."

"Go to Eskiminzin's woman and tell her that Eskiminzin is lying hurt where the lightning-blasted pine points to sentry rock. But as a sign so that she will accept your message, sing the chant that I just taught you."

"All right, I will sing it. But will she know the place?"

"Yes, she will know it. Now hurry!"

I picked up my travois and began pulling it down a short

incline and up the last rise of my journey home. As I plodded along I sang the chant, and it seemed to lighten my load as I walked.

Down into the village I trekked, pulling the travois and singing at the top of my lungs, as best I could. Not just one or two villagers, but the whole village seemed to gather as I dragged in my load. Mother was standing in front of her lodge so I dropped the buffalo at her feet. She looked pleased. But I didn't stop there, I merely stepped out of the travois and kept walking and singing.

Straight to Eskiminzin's lodge I walked, and the closer I got the louder I sang. His woman was standing at the entrance, mouth open in astonishment. Her eyes were red as if she had been crying. When I reached her, I stopped chanting and seated myself cross-legged on the earth directly in front of her, and waited for her to invite me to speak.

"Do...do y-you have something to say, White Thunder?"

"I met a grandmother by the way as I drug my meat home. She taught me the chant I was singing, and sent me to you with a message."

By then most of the village had gathered.

"What is the message?"

"She said to go to you and tell you that Eskiminzin is lying hurt where the lightning-blasted pine points to sentry rock. She said you would know the place."

"I know the place," she said, and started weeping. As I mentioned, her eyes were red, and it was clear she had been crying before I arrived. "I knew Eskiminzin was hurt," she added, "else he would have come home last night or the night before."

"We know the place, too," replied a choir of grandfathers. Warriors headed for their lodges to get their equipment. It was clear that no one questioned the source of my message.

But as they left, old Beyotas, the clan leader and peace chief, turned on his heels and asked as an afterthought, "Where did you learn the chant? I haven't heard it since I was a boy."

"The old grandmother who gave me the message taught it to me as a sign for you. Apparently you know it?"

"Oh yes. Eskiminzin's grandmother used to sing it a lot. What did the old woman look like?"

"She looked much like your women, Beyotas, except that she had a thinner face and a long scar on her left cheek."

"It sound like Eskiminzin's grandmother. She was clawed by a bear when she was small."

• • •

A group of villagers found Eskiminzin exactly where the old woman said he would be. A boulder had fallen on his legs and he was pinned. Only one leg was broken, but he had many abrasions.

When they got him home, his woman continued to weep, but this time for joy. But not a word was said to me. No words of thanks. Nothing.

It was many moons before I learned from Towhee that Shi-Be had arrived in the village a day ahead of me with reports that I practiced witchcraft, and had stirred up some of the villagers. But the next day I came in with the message about Eskiminzin. So the village elders circulated word to everyone to leave me strictly alone, saying that time would tell if I practiced witchcraft or was favored by the gods.

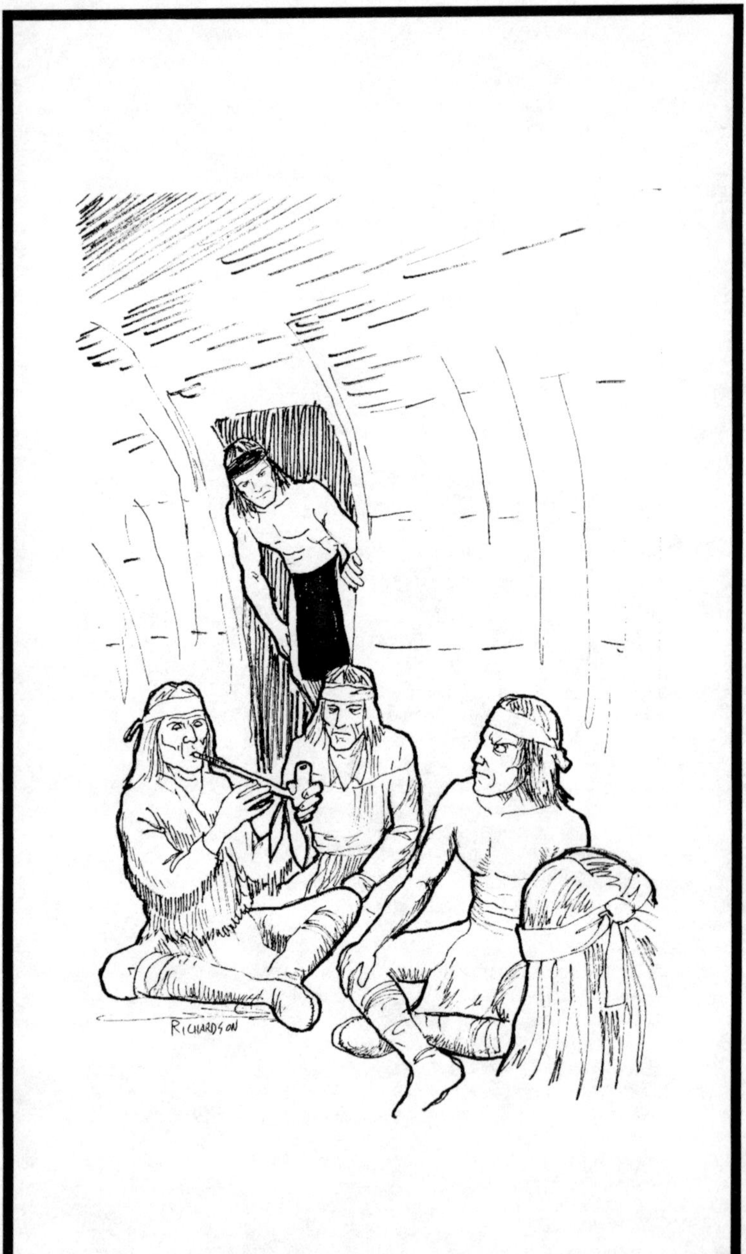
RICHARDSON

The Ponies

I sat in front of Mother's wickiup, wrapped to the waist in a buffalo robe and enjoying the long rays of the southern sun. Under the robe I wore the traditional clout and high moccasins of my heritage. On the peaks around me there was snow, but in our hanging valley the snow was quickly melting, except for the places where the sun didn't reach.

A hundred wickiups or more, exactly like Mother's, were clustered on the sunny side of the valley around me, with the steep south slope of the mountain acting as a heat reflector. In a conspicuous spot nearby was a council lodge which provided for the lodging of the warriors when mothers-in-law came to visit their daughters.

It was early spring, my sixteenth, and the fourth spring for our village in the hanging valleys. Here we were safe and secure while all around us Apache bands and clans were skirmishing with the Spaniards, Navajos, Pueblos, Yaqui, and each other. They claim to follow Child of Water and Killer of Enemies, the gods of war, but when you get the fighting spirit in your craw, you're just like the bug tribe that torments all other tribes. There is always someone to accommodate you for a fight.

Our little village was different from the rest, according to the wandering shaman, Kokopelli, who teaches us to live in harmony with each other and with Earth Woman. He doesn't live with us all the time. One day he will be here and the next day he'll be gone. It's strange how he comes and goes, even in the dead of winter; I suppose that only Earth Mother and Ysun know how he does it.

Lost in thought my eyes wandered to Butterfly Catcher's lodge, where Towhee lived. Tied to a post in front of the lodge were two ponies. I had seen the ponies before, being led by Sieber, son of Shi-Be. At the time I had wondered where he had gotten such fine ponies.

All of a sudden an unthinkable thought struck me that was so awful that I shuttered. My back seemed to snap my whole body to a ridged sitting position without any conscious effort on my part.

The ponies were a marriage proposal for Towhee!

It couldn't be! It just couldn't! A fly could have flown into my open mouth and taken over. Since I had become aware that Towhee was growing into her womanhood, I had hoped that some day I could take her a fine pony, let alone two! Surely she wouldn't accept the proposal, would she?

Heart broken and sick, I could have kicked myself for not acting sooner, for being so backward when it came to talking to girls. But I have nothing to offer. I'm not a fierce, mean fighter that has earned an eagle feather nor am I a great scout or warrior. I'm just I. I can stalk any animal, can slip up to a deer while feeding and slap him on the rump, but I have never killed a human being or done anything extraordinary and honorable.

I looked down, studying the bare ground without saying anything. *I should have done something, but instead I did nothing, thinking she would understand my intentions. But what am I anyway? I am nothing!*

A shadow crossed my face and I looked up into Eskiminzin's eyes. "Was I talking out loud?" I asked.

"You weren't saying words," Eskiminzin said, "but you were communicating."

Eskiminzin seated himself in the spring sunshine beside me, and we sat in silence, the Apache way. A breeze slid through the pines whispering softly in passing, and overhead an eagle soared. Both meant nothing to me.

For a long time we sat in silence, then I envisioned the unspoken question, "What shall I do?"

"We could use meat," Eskiminzin replied softly, as if I had spoken out loud. "Maybe you could go hunting."

Nodding a reply, I arose and made my way to a container of animal fat, which I smeared on my upper torso to provide warmth when I left the shelter of the valley. Then I snatched my bow and quiver from the wickiup and turned to go.

"While you are hunting, I will speak with Butterfly Catcher for you, if you like," the old man volunteered. Butterfly Catcher is Towhee's mother. In order to ask a girl to marry you, you first have to get permission from her mother. It's not the groom that requests permission, but a family member or friend. In other words, Eskiminzin was telling me that he would seek permission for me to ask Towhee to marry me before she married Sieber. But that was absurd, as I didn't have ponies as a proposal gift.

"But I don't have anything for a proposal gift. Where did Sieber get the ponies?"

Eskiminzin shrugged. "From a raid, of course."

"But…" What I was going to say didn't get said because I knew the answer. I was going to say that Kokopelli was discouraging warriors from raiding, but even as the words were forming in my mind I knew that Shi-Be and his sons were not careful followers of the old shaman.

"Before our people used ponies as a proposal gift, they used almost anything of value," Eskiminzin spoke slowly. I cast him a wondering glance as I left the lodge, curious yet discouraged at his words. I didn't have anything of value. Not one thing!

"Remember Enos," Eskiminzin muttered behind me. Enos was an ancestor who went into the forest to hunt, but spent the day envisioning a prayer to Ysun instead. He got an answer, too, and through it taught his descendents the secret of prayer by envisioning.

Passing Butterfly Catcher's lodge, I cast a quick glance at the two ponies standing there, both mares. Movement caught my eye in the lodge entrance and from a distance I could see that it was Towhee, studying me.

Embarrassed, I ducked my head and slipped between two wickiups, toe first, the way I always walked. Towhee says I glide like a cat when I walk, as if I were stalking an animal, even when I'm just walking across the village.

Into the mountain I went; it didn't matter where. I didn't follow the path of least resistance, but the path of frustration up treacherous rocks and ridges. If I fell, so what!

Up high the snow was crunchy and crusted, hiding dangerous holes. Over the crusted snow was a skiff of fresh stuff, soft and slick.

You don't hide your footprints in the snow, so everyone's coming and goings are open for all to see. In a high valley I saw where a mouse had scurried across a patch of snow. An owl had tried to pounce on the little creature but had missed, leaving claw marks in the snow. Owls don't make it a habit of missing, but sometimes a mouse will catch the owl's shadow or the swish of a wing in flight. Or maybe the mouse could smell brother owl. Regardless, the little creature suddenly darted to the side, making for a boulder where the snow had melted back the width of a thumb, leaving a crack for the mouse to scurry into.

As I watched, snow crumbled into the crack—a large chunk as big as a fist—then another. I hesitated to get too close because clearly there was a hole underneath, yet I was curious. Securing a stick, I inched closer to the hole and poked the stick in, widening the hole.

The minute I saw the brown fur, I knew what it was—a silver-tip (grizzly bear), deep in hibernation. Straining my eyes I caught sight of the furry face, his eyes closed in slumber. His muzzle was lighter than the rest of his fur, characteristic of the grizzly bears in our area.

Slowly I backed away. I had no argument with brother bear and would leave him asleep. My people don't even harvest bears for food, as do some more primitive tribes, because bears are too close of a relative to man.

• • •

It was dark when I made my way back to the village, bringing home a yellow-haired porcupine for the cooking pot. As I entered the village I glanced at Towhee's lodge, then looked again.

The ponies were gone!

Clearly Towhee had accepted Sieber's proposal.

Still moping and sick at heart, I dragged my tired frame home to Mother's lodge. Meeting me in the entrance, Mother just stood there, studying me. I thrust the game at her, but she didn't move. Catching my eye she asked, "Do you want to talk about it?"

"About what?" I asked.

"About whatever's bothering you."

"It shows?" I asked.

"Like blood on snow."

"There isn't anything to talk about, Mother. I just need to grow up a little."

"It's about Towhee, isn't it?"

"Uh-huh."

"She was over here when the sun was three or four hands high, and brought this for you," Mother said, thrusting a hunk of perfectly spun cordage at me. Its use was clear, as it was the size and style of a bowstring. It was like her, bringing me gifts she had made, but why would she bring me a present on the day she had accepted a proposal of marriage?

Taking the bowstring, I fingered it reverently, searching Mother's eyes for answers. A gentle smile crossed her face, followed by an amused smile.

"You weren't in the village today, White Thunder, so you don't know what has happened."

"What has happened?"

"Towhee rejected Sieber's proposal."

"But Mother, I saw with my own eyes that the ponies had been cared for."

"The younger generation doesn't always follow the old customs, White Thunder. Towhee went to Sieber and told him to come remove the ponies. She didn't want them standing there unfed for four days and she didn't want to marry him."

I just stood there, too shocked to do anything as Mother relieved me of the porcupine. I walked outside, deep in thought, and absentmindedly wandered over to the council lodge where a fire was going. Several men had gathered to hash over the doings of the day as they passed a pipe filled with a mixture of tobacco and the inner bark of red willow.

On the other side of the circle was Sieber. Briefly our eyes met and I was shocked at what I saw.

Hatred!

I had been raised with Sieber, and possibly understood him even more than his parents understood him. But never before had I saw that look in his eye. The Sieber I was looking at was all warrior, ready to kill, and possessed with Child of Water (a war god)!

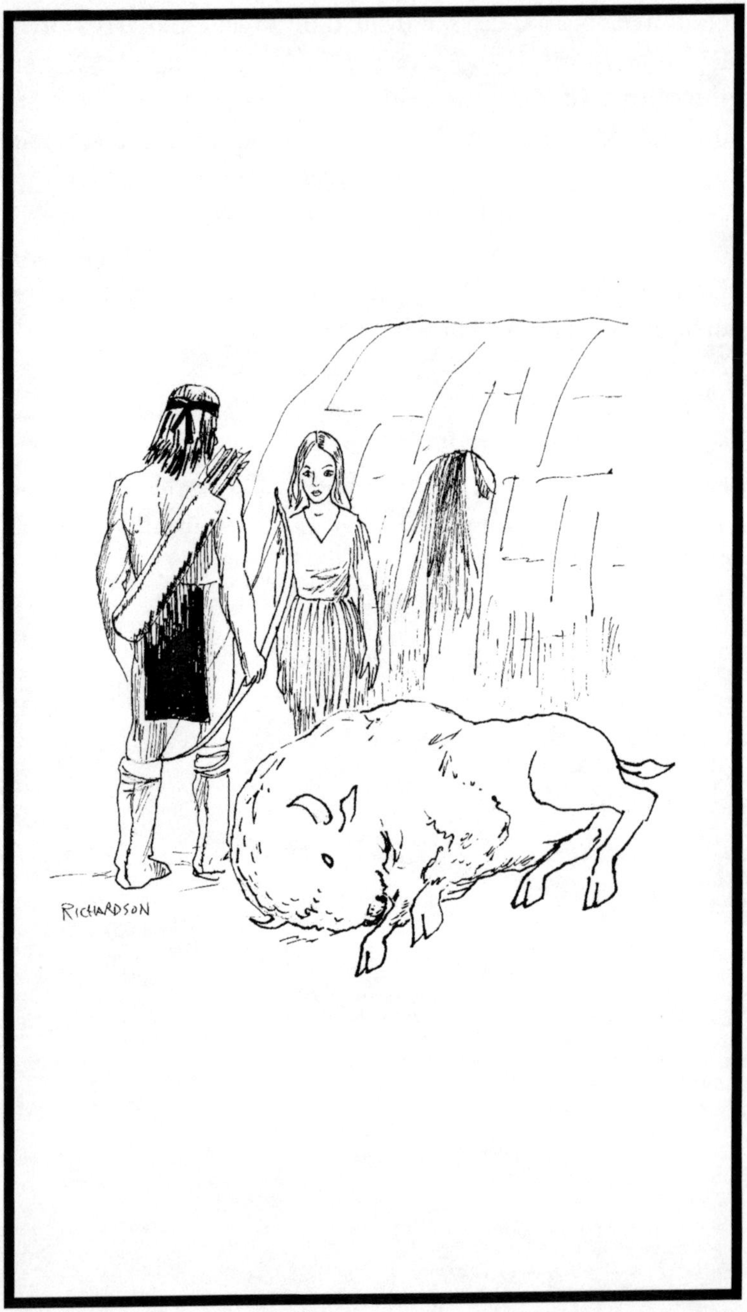
RICHARDSON

Silver-Tip

Old Eskiminzin with thick powerful shoulders and a barrel chest studied the fir tree across the little valley. Gnarled and deformed, the tree managed to eke out a height of forty or fifty feet despite Wind Maker's relentless tormenting. Yet it didn't seem to be the tree alone that interested the old man but the moral it represented.

Ever since I had been the messenger for the ghost of his grandmother, telling the villagers where Eskiminzin lay trapped, he had treated me differently, often playing the role of a grandfather. I knew he had something on his mind, so I waited patiently for him to come out with it.

"You say there is a silver-tip up there in the cave?" he asked.

"I don't know about a cave, but there's a silver-tip bear hibernating in a hole up in the rocks," I replied.

"From the way you described it, it's a cave, White Thunder, but has been walled up to keep the animal tribe from disturbing the home of the old ones. The wall is an arm's length in from the entrance, and I guess the bear is taking advantage of the recess."

"Why would anyone wall up a cave? Unless," I added, "it is a burial cave, which sounds highly unusual."

"It is a burial cave. I studied it out one day and envisioned bodies inside, two of them. They each had tiny yellow metal leaves bound with rings on their chest."

Some of the grandfathers of my people have developed the ability to visualize themselves being somewhere else, often somewhere they had never been. They could capture the sounds and odors, even the spirits of the plants and animals, and tell you everything about a place they have never seen. Grandfather had that ability. So when old Eskiminzin said that he envisioned two bodies in a walled-up cave, I believed him.

"They must be very old bodies," I commented, "because our people usually use crevices for the shells of our dead."

"I don't know how old they are, but Kokopelli knows about them."

"He does? Whom did he say they were?"

"He didn't say who they were, but he said the yellow metal leaves contain a religious ceremony."

"Regardless, I don't want to go anywhere around the place now that I know it is a burial cave."

"Maybe you don't and maybe you do, White Thunder. Bears are our brothers and maybe a talk with brother bear will do you some good?"

"I don't know. Grandfather used to talk with bears, but he

used to do a lot of things that I can't do."

"Look at the fir tree across the valley, Grandson. What would have happened to it if it had given up as easily as you are giving up on Towhee?"

"Giving up? Eskiminzin, I have nothing!"

"In my day, White Thunder, many things made an honorable proposal gift. Of course, that was before ponies were easily had." He cast me a sidewise glance, probably wondering if I caught the suggestion. I had. Fact is, I had already thought of it.

Mind racing, I cast Eskiminzin a questioning glance.

"Maybe Lupin will go with you and give you courage enough to speak with brother bear," he said, meaning Nantan Lupin, my brother-in-law.

"Thanks, Eskiminzin," I replied, rising to my feet.

I had seen Nantan Lupin in the lodge of the warriors, as Mother, his mother-in-law, had gone to visit her daughter, Laughing Grass. So Nantan Lupin had politely left the lodge to the women. Someone had brewed up a small batch of *tulapai* from the meager stores of corn, and the warriors were sharing the drink, as far as it went. *Tulapai* is a mildly alcoholic drink made from dried corn sprouts, weeds, roots, root bark, and a dash of dried loco weed. My people traditionally cannot hold our alcohol and Kokopelli strongly talks against the beverage. Kokopelli is much more successful at talking the villagers into some things than others.

Hunkered down beside a dying fire, longingly studying the empty earthen jugs that had once contained *tulapai*, Nantan Lupin chewed on a mouthful of pine gum. Once you put a chew of pine gum in your mouth, you don't talk much because when you open your mouth to speak, the gum begins to crystallize and has to be spit out. So of necessity it had to be a one-sided conversation.

"Nantan Lupin, would you be willing to go with me? I know where a silver-tip is, and Eskiminzin thinks a good old-fashioned man-to-bear conversation will do me good. Yet he thinks I ought not be alone in case the bear isn't in a conversational mood."

"A silver-tip?" he replied in surprise. I grinned as he realized he had allowed air to touch his pine gum, so he spit it out.

"Uh-huh," I replied.

"And you're going to wake him up and talk with him?"

"We," I corrected him softly, as others were listening, "but maybe he won't be asleep."

"Well, we best get going," he grinned a resolve. "It's near the season for bears to be climbing out of their holes."

• • •

Early the next morning we began climbing steadily, then leveled off and skirted the outcropping of rock. We made our way to the mouth of the burial cave, where I had seen the bear. My generation had lost faith in some of the practices that the older generation held sacred, so I wasn't sure a conversation with brother bear was something I wanted to do. Still I proceeded, more or less blindly following old Eskiminzin's counsel. One thing I didn't do was tell Nantan Lupin that behind the silver-tip was a burial cave. I figured it was something he didn't need to know.

A few hundred steps short of the bear's den, Nantan Lupin seated himself on a rock to wait for me, so all alone I worked my way to the hibernating animal. Then I carefully widened the hole so that I could see the face of the sleeping bear.

"Bear Brother," I began, "listen to my words."

Of course the silver-tip paid me no mind because he was

sleeping, and I puzzled over my problem. If I woke him up he would be angry, and I wasn't sure that it was polite to go into a bear's den and wake him. But if I didn't wake him, how could I talk to him?

Can you envision a communication with a sleeping animal? I thought not, but I tried, envisioning a message of my desire for Towhee, and asking for his counsel. Still the silver-tip slept and my envisioned message seemingly went unnoticed.

"This won't work," I muttered to myself as I glanced back to where Nantan Lupin sat, waiting for me. Surely old silver-tip knew where I could find an offering suitable for a proposal gift for Towhee, and had he been awake I might have been able to envision a communication with him. But he was asleep.

I glanced down at the bear, then looked again. His head had moved slightly, though still he slept.

Should I try again to communicate? I thought not.

Gathering my feet under me, I rose to my feet and scanned the mountain side. As I did, my mind drifted away to a tiny hanging valley lower down on the mountain side, but not as low as the valley where our village was. In my mind I saw an old buffalo that had gone off to die all by itself last fall, and was frozen in the snow.

It was a vision of a sort, and when it closed I glanced at old Silver-Tip. "Are you trying to communicate with me?" I asked. The bear just slept on.

Returning to Nantan Lupin, I told him of my vision, asking him if he thought it was real or just the imagination of a warrior with an empty head.

"One way to find out," he replied. "Where did you say the valley was?"

"I'll show you," I replied. "But even if there is an old frozen buffalo there, what good will it do us?"

"If nothing else, it will give us some frozen meat."

We started out with the sun about to hide behind some thin clouds, which thickened as the day wore on. Though we couldn't see the sun, we traveled about the length of time it would have taken Father Sun to move two hands, coming onto the valley from the uphill side.

"Where did you vision the buffalo?" Nantan Lupin asked.

"On the sunrise side," I stated after long moments of thought. "We'll have to use our bows as sticks to poke down through the snow to find the carcass."

Nantan Lupin just grunted as he unstrung his bow. Moving to the sunrise side of the tiny valley, we started poking our bows into the snow, trying to locate something. The clouds had turned dark and the skies began to look angry when for the dozenth time my bow struck what felt like a boulder. As I had done a dozen times already, I dug down with my hands, but this time it wasn't stone that I uncovered, but the thick coat of a buffalo. Not just any buffalo, but a spotted medicine buffalo. A spotted buffalo is highly prized, and considered good medicine.

I could hardly believe it!

Calling to Nantan Lupin, who was only a short distance away, I began scrambling to uncovering the beast completely. By the time the task was completed, Nantan Lupin was looking over my shoulder.

"Thank you, Brother Buffalo, for the gift of your flesh and bones. May your spirit go to the clouds with our ancestors," I prayed. It was a prayer of thanks, one customary of our village. When you use the body of any animal, you should thank the animal for the use of his body—it's only polite. Yet to me it was more than polite, it was heart felt words of gratitude.

"That was too easy," Nantan Lupin observed. "The villagers will never believe it. Do you want me to create a story about how the old monarch charged you as you stood defenseless with nothing to kill him with but your bare hands? I could describe how you wrestled the beast to the ground, barehanded."

Nantan Lupin's voice sounded so serious that I had to glance up to see the humor in his eyes.

"How would I explain the frozen carcass?" I replied in much the same tone as my brother-in-law.

"Well then," Nantan Lupin replied, "maybe I could tell them that you did it last week."

"Maybe we should just tell the truth."

"You sure make it hard for a brother-in-law to have an interesting story to tell around the fire at night," he complained. "You get me to help with all the backbreaking work but don't give me any good stories to tell. What kind of a brother-in-law are you anyway?"

I grinned. "We do have a problem, though, Nantan Lupin. We don't want to drag the beast home wrapped in his own hide and take a chance on damaging the only spotted buffalo hide I have ever seen."

"You have a point there, White Thunder. What do you suggest?"

"Now that the carcass is exposed, it will have to be guarded from prowling meat eaters. So why don't I guard the carcass while you get some help from the village? We will also need an old hide to slide the carcass home upon."

Nantan Lupin nodded. "While at the village, should I tell Towhee about the medicine hide?" He was teasing, of course. I just looked at him, giving him my most exasperated look. He got the point. "Just asking," he replied, "but I can see you want me to do all the work and have none of the fun."

∙ ∙ ∙

Turning on his heels, Nantan Lupin started back to the village for help. While waiting, I would have started cleaning the animal, were he not frozen. But even if it had been a fresh kill, you don't want to clean an animal if you can help it because when you clean the animal, you lose entrails while dragging the animal home, and all parts of an animal can be used. One of the most useful parts are the intestines, which are cut into small sections and roasted on a stick over low coals, then eaten as a great treat. So I just waited.

It seemed like a long time before men from the village came over the ridge. They were in good spirits and awestruck by the animal's spotted coat. But Nantan Lupin had shared with them my experience of envisioning a conversation with the old silver-tip, in accordance with old Eskiminzin's counsel.

With many hands the work went quickly. Still we were totally exhausted before I reached the village.

∙ ∙ ∙

Dogs barked and children gawked as we dragged the heavy beast into the village. Literally everyone came to the entrance of their lodges, if not all the way out. Most of the villagers, including myself, had never seen a spotted buffalo before. It was considered more than a great trophy; it was good medicine. Additionally, the animals represented much food, food that would be shared by all because in an Apache village, if one family has food, everyone has food.

Dragging the animal across the village to Butterfly Catcher's lodge, we were aware that all eyes were on us. As old Eskiminzin had said, before ponies became a gift appropriate for a marriage proposal, anything rare was a gift. Nothing was rarer than a spotted buffalo, unless it was a white buffalo, and nobody in the village had actually seen a white buffalo.

Marriage proposal gifts are supposed to be left at the lodge where the girl lives at night. But when the gift was a gift of meat that had to be cared for, it was not practical to leave it during the dark hours of night.

Towhee stood in the door way, gawking at the buffalo and at those of us who were dragging the heavy carcass. Over her shoulder we could see Butterfly Catcher, equally as interested in what we were doing. With all watching, I was hard pressed to keep a straight face.

Dragging the carcass the remainder of the way to Butterfly Catcher's lodge, we all released our holds on the creature. I couldn't help but look up, and when I did, I was looking eye to eye with Towhee. Realization was beginning to set in as she realized that the buffalo was a proposal gift. Taking advantage of her close proximity, I envisioned a message of love and hope to her. Then I pivoted on my moccasins, thanked the men that helped me drag the animal home, and struck a course across the village for Mother's lodge. As I passed Eskiminzin, sitting at the entrance to his woman's lodge, he caught my eye. No words were expressed, but he flashed me a look of triumph.

Curiosity caused me to cast a departing glance over my shoulder toward Towhee, and what I saw caused my heart to leap within me.

Towhee was preparing to butcher the animal without hesitation!

Smiling to myself, though outwardly more reserved, I was pleased. Yet for no conscious reason whatsoever, I glanced to Sieber's mother's lodge, and caught the rejected suitor starring at me. For just a minute our eyes met, and what I saw I didn't like.

The Rhythm of a Lullaby Chant

The cadence of the ceremonial drums nearly made the mountainside rock. Earth Mother is very much alive, and has a pulse of her own, something like the beating of a heart, and the rhythm of the ceremonial drums helps that cadence come to life. The drummers were using Apache water drums—watertight drums partly filled with water until they gave of a particular pitch.

Mother sat alone in the rocks overlooking the village, rocking slowly to the rhythm of a lullaby chant. The village had been feasting for three days, or at least feasting as much as they could on the meager meat available in the early spring. It was the traditional Apache wedding feast for Towhee and me, and a feast of triumph for Butterfly Catcher, who was gaining another provider in the family.

But mother sat alone in thought, probably pleased that her son was marrying high in the community, but knowing that it was all over for her. After all, when you have a daughter in the Apache culture, you have her for life, but when you have a son, he is only yours until he finds a wife. The family of the groom becomes little more than just another family in the village, and a new wickiup is built for the happy couple next to the lodge of the bride's mother.

The songs Mother chanted were the cradle chants of my childhood—lullabies that I had known all my life. From where I stood, not far away, I could see an index finger ring a hole in the front of her buckskin dress and the rays of sunlight caught trails of moisture trickling down her cheeks.

Climbing the last few rocks remaining as I made my way to her, we sat together and looked over the view. A rock marmot pocked his head out and rolled its eyes at us. Maybe it was the marmot's first trip from his den of hibernation for the spring, as it looked gaunt and sleepy-eyed. After studying us for a short time, he gave his shrill whistle call, and disappeared into the rocks once more.

"You should not be here, White Thunder. A mother should be alone to meditate the past."

"Sometimes it helps to be alone, Mother, but there will be time for that."

We talked of my babyhood crawling around the lodge, and of the pride Mother, Father, and Grandfather took in me. Some memories were sweet, others bittersweet, such as my first conditioning run in the cold. I had not realized that my first run would affect Mother so much. Fact is, I hadn't realized she knew so much about it.

The morning of that run was cold, but not too cold for it to snow. Grandfather and I were a long way from our village, up in the mountain, and we had spent the night in a leaf lodge with a stack of leaves atop us as high as Grandfather's arm. As we sat around the fire in the morning, I let the shivers get to me, but Grandfather sat there as if it were a warm spring day.

"Aren't you cold, Grandfather?" I murmured between chatters of my teeth.

"I would be cold if I fought it as you are doing, Grandson. Cold is our friend, but you are treating it as if it were an enemy."

"I know cold keeps the insect population down and keeps our meat from spoiling, but I can't help it, Grandfather. I'm still shivering. How can you sit there without shivering?"

"I will teach you how to do it, Grandson. Take off all your clothes, all but your clout and we will stash them in the branches of this tree."

"But Grandfather, I'll freeze."

"If you freeze, we'll freeze together, because I will be right beside you."

More out of obedience than good sense, I took off my leather shirt and leggings and watched as Grandfather stashed them high in a tree, along with his shirt and leggings. Then together we started running home, nearly a half days slow run away.

It was snowing, large beautiful flakes, and at times there was a little sleet. But as we ran I began to feel the warmth, and soon I realized that Grandfather was playfully tossing snowballs at me as we ran. We started to laugh, both of us, and it was a lot of fun. When we got home, Mother was standing in front of her lodge, waiting for us. How she knew we were coming, I was never told. She gathered me in her arms as if I were a child and held me close, and I liked it. Then she passed both of us some corn cakes, our favorite meal, and listened as I told of our exciting day. Of all their virtues, an Apache mother's best virtue is that she is a good listener.

Since then, Grandfather taught me how to tell my body to be warm in ice cold streams and lakes, and Mother was always there when I got home. It was all part of Grandfather's training, but apparently back in the lodge Mother worried.

As we talked, I was impressed for the first time by how much heartache was expended as she turned me over to the care of Grandfather at age seven. Children grow up and are gone, and parents think they can turn their children loose when it is time, but it is hard, especially if they have also lost their spouse. I also began to realize how much she missed Father and Grandfather, and how much she would miss me. At least she had Grandmother and Laughing Grass.

From somewhere came the "Coo-ah, coo, coo, coo" of a brown morning dove. It was as if the bird was telling us that the sun was moving across the sky and we must get busy. So I gathered myself up and left Mother to her thoughts as she sat on the cliff. Her spirits were lifted and we had enjoyed several hours together.

• • •

The third day of the wedding feast was in full swing. Clown man was entertaining everyone at the expense of Towhee, so she was anxious for me to join her and become the blunt of some of the jokes.

As the sun began to flirt with the western peaks, the fire was built up and the dancing commenced. But rather than participate in the dancing, Towhee slipped her hand in mine and we stole away to begin our married life.

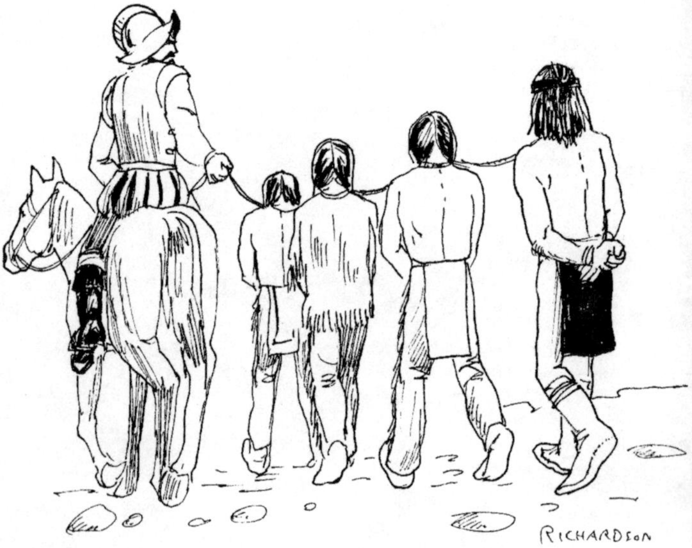
RICHARDSON

A Walk in the Forest

The gentians were in full bloom and tall. I delicately made my way through the field of blue flowers, sidestepping the larger plants. Grandfather was big on insisting that man needs to live at one with nature and not walk all over it. "When a man walks through a meadow," he used to say, "he should not leave a trail as if he were a bear." Grandfather insisted that I make an effort to step over the plants rather than shuffle through them, particularly plants that have medicinal value, as do the gentians.

As I made my way through the field, honey bees were busy going from flower to flower, something I made a mental note of. Where there are bees, there is honey.

High, thin clouds did little to hide the sun as I walked, but the heat felt good. All too soon the snows of winter would be upon us and we would wish for the long days of summer. Even now the squirrels were busy gathering *beyotas* (acorns) and the deer were growing new velvet antlers.

A woodpecker stopped his pecking and a chickadee took gentle flight. Maybe they were both taking notice of my passing, but I wasn't particularly close to either of them. It seemed that I was not alone, yet being so close to our village and having others around was no reason to fall to the forest floor and probably damage a few gentians as I slithered to the safety of undergrowth.

"Why do you walk alone in the forest, White Thunder?" Sieber spoke as he appeared from under a buckbrush bush. Sieber had been standoffish toward me ever since Towhee and I were wed, and it seemed good to once again be in the woods with my boyhood friend—just he and I and Earth Woman.

"I am generally alone as I hunt, these days, Sieber, but I welcome your company."

"You misunderstand, White Thunder. You will not continue to have my company."

"What do you mean?"

Suddenly someone caught me from behind in a bear hug. Whomever it was, he was a bull of a man. Sieber stepped forward and started tying one wrist with leather straps, and in no time at all he pulled the wrist behind my back and tied it to the other wrist. I was confused, really confused, but as I searched Sieber's face it showed nothing. He wouldn't even look directly at me. As it turned out, the bull of a man behind me was none other than Shi-Be.

"What is the meaning of this?" I demanded. "I thought we were friends, Sieber!"

"We were friends until you persuaded Towhee to return my ponies and marry you. You knew that I had been in love with her all her life."

"No, I didn't know that. I knew that I was in love with her, but you never talked about Towhee in a romantic way. Besides, even if you were in love with her, it was me who she chose. And I didn't persuade her to return your ponies; I didn't even speak with her about it until after it was all over. But I am glad she did because I have wanted to marry her since she began her womanhood."

"She only returned the ponies because you cast some type of a witchcraft spell on her. She would have never left me for you without it."

"You take yourself too seriously, Sieber. Apparently she did."

"Yes, but under your spell."

"I do not use witchcraft, Sieber, and you know it!"

"I do not know it, White Thunder. I think you do."

"Don't look White Lighting in the eye, Sieber," Shi-Be broke in. "He'll bewitch you. Believe me, I know!" Sieber followed his father's council, keeping his eyes on the ground.

"Regardless of what you think of me, what are you going to do?" I asked. "Why have you tied my wrists behind my back as if I were an enemy?"

"You are an enemy, White Thunder. You used to be a boyhood friend, but when you took Towhee from me, you became an enemy."

"So what are you going to do with me?" I asked a little more slowly, suspiciously.

"We are not going to kill you, if that is what you are asking. After all, we were raised together. But we have a use for you. When you are gone, your witchcraft spell over Towhee will leave and she will come to her senses."

"Don't count on it, Sieber."

He glared at me. "I am counting on it, White Thunder."

"You still haven't said what you are going to do with me."

"No, we haven't, but you don't need to know. You'll learn soon enough."

• • •

We made our way out of the mountains, traveling south by southeast. At night we slept near a grove of sycamore trees. Sieber and Shi-Be were both uneasy and slept very little. I didn't sleep well either, as I was uncomfortable with my hands tied behind my back, and sick with worry over what might happen to Towhee with me out of the way.

Toward midday we climbed a prominent rise and seated ourselves under a cypress tree. Apparently Shi-Be and Sieber were waiting for someone. The sun was hot and the heat of the day was in full bloom. Even the red ants had gone into their ant hills. Only a dumb scorpion was out to absorb the day's heat, and it quickly sought the shade of a rock.

The sun had traveled one, maybe two hands when they came riding in: two men, leading three others on leashes that were tied around the captives' necks. Right off I knew the men weren't likely to be Apaches, as they were riding horses.

The two men that were riding horses both had dark features, and as they drew closer I saw that one was Cat Whiskers, the man I had seen a year earlier conversing with Shi-Be. Even as I watched he broke into a fit of coughing, and it surprised me that after nearly a year his sickness hadn't gone away.

I didn't know Cat Whisker's companion, but the three men on leashes were clearly Navajos. The pieces of the puzzle were beginning to fit together.

Slaves!

My old boyhood friend and his father were selling me as a slave to the Spanish!

I glanced from Shi-Be to Sieber. Shi-Be's face shown with triumph, but Sieber was studying the ground. "How could you?" I asked. I really didn't expect an answer and didn't get one.

Leaving the Navajo prisoners to the care of Cat Whiskers, his companion rode up the rise to meet us. Bucking his mount to a stop, he seemed to take pleasure in the dust choking us.

"My name is Delgadito," he announced in Apache, as if the mere mention of his name should inspire fear or respect in us. Delgadito means slim one, which described the man perfectly.

Shi-Be seemed unimpressed, I'll have to grant him that. He just looked Delgadito in the mouth, true Apache style, and said, "So?"

"You She-Bee, no?"

"No, the name is not She-Bee, it's Shi-Be, and if you had any skill with the Apache language, you would have known how to pronounce it."

Clearly Shi-Be had called Delgadito's bluff. Maybe he was a big man where he came from, but not in the middle of the desert. Then Shi-Be seated himself cross legged on the ground with all the dignity of a chief, and waited for Delgadito to follow. It took a moment or two, but Delgadito finally gave in, swinging to the ground. Clearly Shi-Be and Sieber didn't trust Delgadito all the way because I noticed that Sieber had an arrow fit conveniently to his bowstring for quick use.

Slowly, Delgadito untied a package from behind his saddle and seated himself opposite Shi-Be. Opening the package it contained some red cloth, a knife, and an iron tomahawk.

Dickering dragged on for a long time, and Cat Whiskers,

maybe an eighth of a mile away, was clearly growing uneasy. Before the conversation was over, Shi-Be had the cloth, knife, tomahawk, and a necklace from around Delgadito's neck. I didn't know I was worth so much. That made Shi-Be a rich man. His squaw would sing his praises when he got back to the village with the riches, but I wondered where Shi-Be would say they came from.

Ambling over, Delgadito tied a leash around my neck and led me down the hill to the other captives. I was tied at the rear of the string of prisoners, but my hands were still tied behind my back the remainder of the day, while the other prisoners' hands were tied in front.

As we moved out, I glanced up the rise at Sieber, my boyhood-friend-turned-enemy. What would happen to me? What would happen to Towhee, the wife I would never see again?

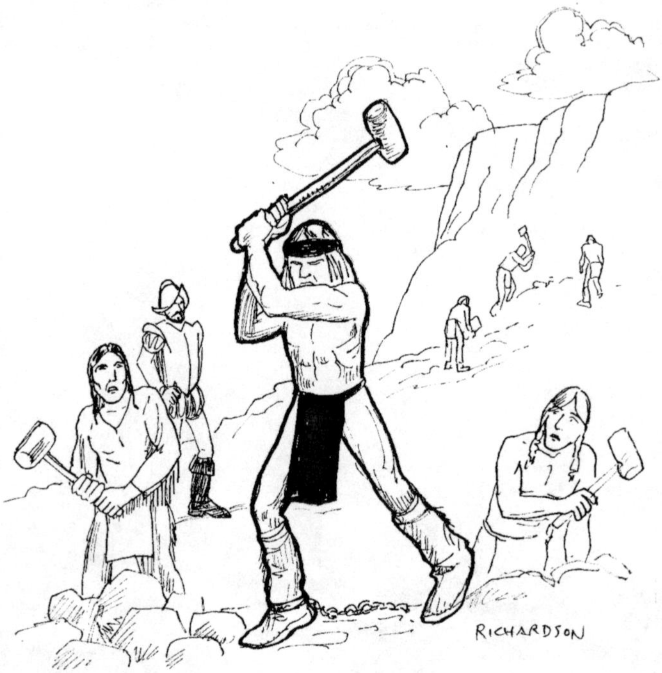
RICHARDSON

In For Hard Times

Hour after hour we plodded south through the dusty desert. Clearly Cat Whiskers or Delgadito, whoever was choosing the route, lacked skill in desert travel. Even as a boy I could have found water in the desert, but we were walking waterless across the most inhospitable portion of the desert, passing chances for water on both sides. Nor did they seem to know about the water-bearing cacti.

Ocotillo and senita cacti were everywhere, ready to snag anyone who walked too close to them. We didn't travel in a straight line, but wandered around somewhat, as if the leaders weren't sure of the route. Then we came onto a somewhat flat desert floor, thick with cholla and saguaro cacti. We turned west. The scorching sun beat down like an evil enemy, cooking us as we walked.

It was then that Delgadito fitted all of us captives with blindfolds, making us stumble along in cue between the thorny cacti as best we could. Four days into our trip we turned north again and entered steep mountains, thick with cacti. Fact is, the cacti was so thick that we slowed down Cat Whiskers and Delgadito enough that they removed our blindfolds for faster travel.

I smelled the water before we reached it, and so did the horses. It was a tiny intermittent stream, high in the mountains, but not high enough to be out of the cacti. On the banks of the stream were a dozen horses and mules, and an equal number of Spanish soldiers. A handful of scrawny, undernourished slaves were crushing rocks with hammers and picking out the yellow metal. The slaves were clearly Apache, but of a clan with which I was unfamiliar. So emancipated were they that they were talking skeletons.

From a gaping hole in Earth Woman, slaves occasionally brought out loads of fresh rock to be crushed, and a quarter mile away was a smelter where other slaves labored. Life began to look dark and scary.

The soldiers greeted Delgadito and Cat Whiskers with less-than-glowing enthusiasm. Clearly there was no love lost between the Spaniards. But if the soldiers lacked love for Delgadito and Cat Whiskers, they had even less for us captives. Without offering us water, food or anything, we were set to work crushing rock. I suspected we were given those tasks without first being offered water so that they could see what manner of workers we were.

It was late in the day, so there were only a few hours of sunlight left in the sky. We worked those few hours in near silence, then were taken to the bank of the tiny stream to be bedded down after a meal. The meal consisted of a small squash, roasted whole in the coals, one to a slave.

For work I was teamed up with the three Navajo: Kayenta, Brown Horse, and Chind. The Apache and Navajo languages are almost identical, except that the Navajo speak it so slowly that you get tired waiting for them to complete what they have to say. In the past I have despised the Navajos out of general principle, but thrown together as slaves, we got along very nicely.

In the evenings we had a chance to talk: Kayenta, Brown Horse, Chind and I. We compared the stories we had heard from the other captives, and they weren't promising. Some had been at the mine since it opened three years earlier, and it was said that no one left alive. Everyone was either worked or whipped to death. Of course it was obvious to me that the stories weren't entirely true, as some obviously died of malnutrition.

One thing of great interest to us was that many of the captives lacked toes. It was said that the toes were cut off by the guards to keep the slaves from running away.

Clearly we were in for a hard time, and I would never see Towhee again. Yet with all their cruelty, the Spanish could not top my own people—not my village by Apaches as a whole. Still, Apache torture is finished in a few days while slavery goes on and on.

"Kayenta," I said one day as we paused for a well-deserved drink of water. "It seems to be the consensus of opinion of everyone here, Spanish and Indian alike, that we will be worked to death."

He just grunted, but cast me a look that said *what are you getting at?*

"Why should we stretch the misery of slavery out over so long of a period of time?"

"You thinking of killing yourself?"

"Well, yes and no. How hard do you think you would have to work to kill yourself."

"I don't know. You going to try?"

"I thought I might. I don't like to drag this slow death out over so many years."

• • •

The nip of autumn was in the air as we were roused from our sleep and were given some roasted prickly pear pads for nourishment, then sent to our labors. Arriving a step ahead of the other captives, I chose the largest and heaviest hammer. It was a huge tool with the handle as long as a leg with a heavy head.

Working with a speed I didn't know I had, I put my back and mind into my work. Before long I felt the weakness that comes with fatigue and knew I was on to something. As far as I had been able to tell, the weakness that comes with fatigue is identical to the weakness that comes just before death.

Encouraged, I continued working as fast a pace as I could, feeling my muscles slowly dying within me. The Spaniards were not going to have me as a slave for long. They surely weren't.

There was no hatred for the Spanish within me. As I said, they treated us better than most Apaches treated their captives. Of course our village wasn't like other Apache villages. We didn't take slaves nor did we torture or do a lot of other things that other villagers consider necessary and fun. We were strict followers of Kokopelli, all except for a few, Shi-Be being the most dominate non-follower.

At times I wished for Sieber to work beside me—not the Sieber that sold me to the Spanish as a slave, but the Sieber of my childhood that I played with. As we grew older, we went on long runs together, explored new places, and were hunting companions.

I worried about Towhee, but was sure that Sieber would take good care of her in his own way. I wondered if she was with a child, wondered what she was thinking, and wondered what she was cooking for the evening meal.

At the end of the day I was surprised that I was still alive, but I could feel my muscles dying. All day I had been drinking water, sweating, and working. It wouldn't be long now. Fact is, I might even be dead by the time the sun rose in the morning.

Our usual fare for the evening meal was a roasted squash. When the guard handed me my food, he muttered, "A working man needs a lot of food," as he shoved a large squash my direction. It was a huge squash, double the size of the others. I accepted it mutely, but inwardly knew that it might be my last meal before I died.

In the morning I wasn't dead. I knew right off that I wasn't dead because I arose to the soreness and stiffness of a slave. Grandfather would have told me not to fight the soreness of my muscles, but to work with it, so I welcomed the pain, knowing that it might be my last day on earth.

Again I worked with a vengeance, meaning that I put my back and muscles into my work and didn't slack. To keep my mind off my muscles while I slowly died, I listened to the guards talk, making a game out of it. The game was to guess what they said.

On into the day I worked, drinking great quantities of water and sweating large drops of sweat. Never slacking, always pressing forward in my goal, I kept going.

It was the third day of my attempt to work myself to death that the rattlesnake came. You would think that any dumb rattlesnake knows enough to stay away when he hears the ring of a hammer on rock, but this rattlesnake didn't—he just wandered in. The Navajo slaves just stepped aside, not wanting to bother the messenger from the Underworld, but I was fed up with life, the Underworld, Ysun, everything!

The reptile slithered up toward one of the Spanish guards and did his rattlesnake thing to tell the Spaniard to make way, but the guard paid him no mind. Sometimes Spaniards think they are very high and mighty, or maybe they're just dumb. So the guard just stood there as Brother Rattlesnake curled up and rattled his complaint. The Indians all heard the rattle and paused in their work to watch the guard get bitten. Of course that infuriated the guard, who knew nothing about the messenger from the Underworld.

Well, I could not have cared less about the guard. Nor was I in a mood for much respect for the messenger from the Underworld. Nor did I care if I got bit. It just didn't matter! Fact is, I don't know what got into me except that I did harbor a little concern for the safety of the snake. I surely wasn't concerned for the safety of the guards, that's for sure. Besides, it was a challenge, and I hadn't had many challenges recently.

I slipped up to the rattler, who was intent on the guard, not me. The rattler struck, and so did I, catching the reptile in midair. There are people who say it can't be done, that you can't catch a snake in mid-strike, but I did it.

I whipped up that snake and flung it to the mountain side so quickly that it was all a blur. Some people would have saved the snake for food, but not us Apaches. We Apaches are so peculiar about what we eat—we don't eat pigs, we don't eat birds, we don't eat fish, we don't eat snakes. It's a wonder we eat anything at all except buffalo, deer and elk.

As I said, I flung the snake to the safety of the mountainside, then was suddenly ashamed of myself. The other prisoners looked at me as if I had done something evil in not letting the snake bite the guard.

"You saved the guard's life," I heard from somewhere. I looked up into the face of Delgadito, one of the few Spaniards that spoke Apache.

Concerned, I allowed wrinkles of concern to gather on my forehead, because it had not been my intention to save the life of a guard, of all people, but in doing so, it didn't occur to me to say the incident was anything but what it was. I guess that I had practiced not lying so long that telling the absolute truth was part of my nature. Besides, I would be dead in a few more days. I just knew it. I was about to work myself to death.

Looking deeply into Delgadito's eyes in my most witchcraft fashion—as I no longer feared being accused of using witchcraft—I searched his soul. After a few long moments I spit out my reply.

"Tell the Spanish coyote," I snapped, "that I didn't care if he died. I was saving the life of the messenger from the Underworld."

Delgadito was taken back by my careless statement, and the Indians froze. Dead silence filled the mountain slope. A horse blew, and from somewhere a hawk called.

Slowly Delgadito translated and the guard cast me a hard look. I don't know why the other guards thought it was funny, but suddenly they broke out into laughter which grew in intensity. Soon the contagious laughter drew in some of the prisoners, and all were laughing.

• • •

Autumn slipped into winter and during the winter only us prisoners were comfortable, as we were working hard enough to keep ourselves warm. The guards stood around shivering and fighting the cold—making fools of themselves. Their misery caused some humor among the slaves who thought it was funny that grown men should act like children.

Our food supply increased, but then the Spaniards brought in something they called "salt pork." We were sure they were trying to poison us with the awful, salty stuff, but to our surprise we lived through it. We soon learned that salting meat was the Spaniards' method of preserving it, but what good does it do to preserve food if it renders it so salty that it is inedible?

What amazed me most was that I was still alive. I gave it everything I had to work myself to death and still my muscles were living. Faster and faster, harder and harder I worked, doing the work of several men.

In concentrating of the Spaniard's jabbering to take my mind off my dying muscles, I was learning Spanish. Fact is, I found that I was understanding almost everything they said, though I had yet to speak a word in Spanish.

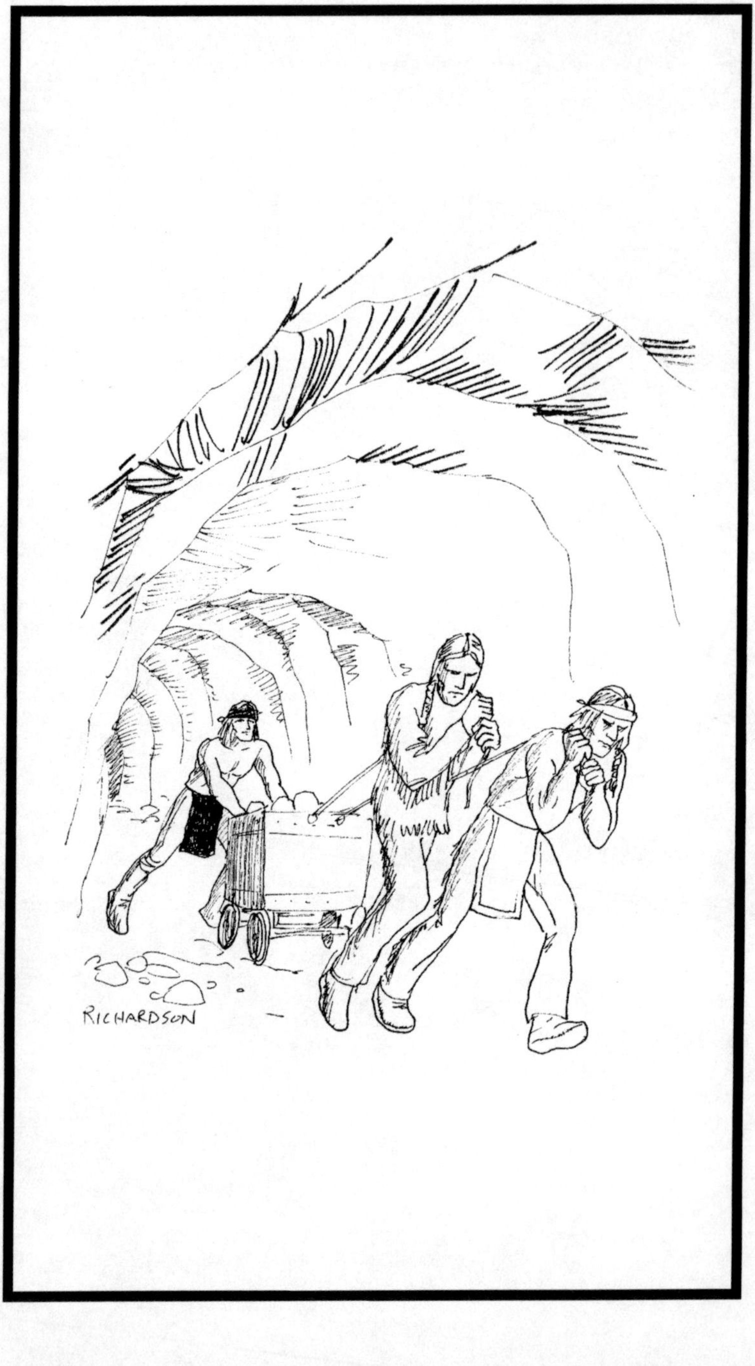
RICHARDSON

Under the Overhang

    The wind whistled through the desert mountain passes and down the canyons. Occasionally it brought snow or sleet, but the snow didn't last. If you were standing around, as were the guards, it chilled your bones, but no slaves were standing around.
    I'll have to hand it to the Spaniards, at least they found food for all. It wasn't necessarily the food we would choose, nor was there a lot of it, but no one starved. Squashes and prickly pears were our mainstays, but other times for a meal we had a small gourd of beans or a small yam, roasted in the fire. Apaches generally eat when there is food and fast when there isn't, but the Spaniards hoarded their food and gave us

just a tiny portion each day. Our stomachs were never full, not even close to being full, but we learned a new way to stretch the winter food supply. I wondered how my village was doing for food, particular Towhee. My mother had Nantan Lupin to hunt for her and Laughing Grass, but who did Towhee have?

Native Americans believe that we are part of Earth Mother—we came from the earth and we will go to the earth when we die. We are brothers to the animals and plants, and if everything is in harmony, we can communicate with the plants and animals. But the Spanish believe that Earth Mother exists for their exploitation. They make deep scars in the mountain for the yellow metal, and care not for the plants and animals. When they partake of the plants, they don't leave a gift for the plant spirits, and when they kill an animal, they don't thank the animal for the gift of his flesh. They are unthankful, unholy, ungodly.

Kokopelli taught our village that Giver of Life and Quetzalcoatl created both Earth Mother and Apaches, along with all the plants and animals. Apaches reverence Earth Mother and the plants and animals, or they displease Giver of Life, and become as unholy as the Spanish.

• • •

In the early spring a supply train arrived with the most unusual contraption you ever saw. The guards called it an ore wagon. Wide as a big man's forearm from his elbow to his finger tips and twice as long, it had round iron things that the guards called wheels. They didn't give any of that information to us slaves, but I was able to understand them as they spoke amongst themselves in Spanish.

The day the ore wagon arrived was the day the huge rock

rolled against Chind, pinning him solid. An ugly guard started whipping him, thinking the whipping would provide enough incentive for him to gather enough muscles to pull himself free. But it doesn't take any brains at all to know that whipping will only work if the slave isn't really stuck, and Chind was clearly pinned. I never did credit most of the guards with a lot of brains. It would appear that if you were a Spaniard and you weren't smart enough to do anything else, they made you a guard.

I figured that if the guard kept whipping Chind like he was doing, he would soon kill the Navajo. Of course it didn't really make much difference if a slave died of whipping or was worked to death, it still made me mad. I slipped right in between Chind and the guard, taking a few blows of the whip, and gathered the huge rock in my arms. In size it was no larger than my chest, but it was really heavy and took all I had to lift it. I gathered the rock in my arms and rolled it close to my chest. Then I straightened to my full height and walked to the edge of the debris area to deposit it. I would have liked to have deposited it on the guard's toe.

When I looked around, several of the guards were cautiously watching me, as were the other slaves. Returning to my rock crushing duties, I wondered what I had done wrong. All afternoon the other slaves cast me questioning sidewise glances.

"Why do the other slaves give me strange looks?" I asked Brown Horse that evening. "Have I done something to offend them?"

Brown Horse grinned, at least the corners of his mouth turned up a little which is as near as he ever came to a grin. "I can't speak for them, White Thunder, but I didn't know that any man alive could lift such a huge rock. Neither did I know that an Apache would come to the rescue of a Navajo. The guard might have killed you." I was a little surprised myself that I went to the rescue of Chind, as in the past I had considered all Navajo as little more than a nuisance.

The next morning one of the guards came to me and announced, "You will push the ore wagon. The mine isn't large enough for our large horses, and you are the strongest slave here. Pick two captives to pull the cart, whomever you choose." When pulling the ore from the mine, a rope was tied to the front of the wagon, but the purpose of the rope was mainly for steering. The rope was nearly strong enough to take the weight of a fully-loaded ore wagon.

For the first time since becoming a slave, I was scared. The mine was a shaft into the Underworld where the darkest of all spirits lurked. Of course we originally all came from the Underworld and would possible go there when we died. Regardless, any spirits, even the spirits of just men, are scary. Where had Kokopelli said the Spirit World was? He hadn't.

Clearly there was a lot that I didn't know nor was it my lot as a slave to choose where I worked. I looked at the entrance of the mine and wondered if I would fit inside. I was taller than most Apaches. I had also gained some height since I had become a slave as well as width in my shoulders.

Chind would be one of the slaves I'd pick, if he was willing to go into the mine, but I was lost as to whom the second could be. There was a man of the Maricopa band named Scorpion that was particularly agile, quick on his feet and with his hands, yet he lacked the strength to crush rock. He seemed like the perfect person to scamper up the mine tunnel, pulling the ore wagon and keeping it steered in the general direction we wanted to go. He was tanking up on water, getting ready for the day's work when I approached him.

"Scorpion, I have been assigned to push the ore wagon full of ore out of the mine. I am to pick two slaves to help pull and steer it. I will choose you and Chind, provided you are both willing to go into the Underworld with me."

Scorpion straightened to his full height, which wasn't very tall. Straightened up as he was, he scarcely reached even my armpits.

"I will follow you, Grandfather, if you want me."

"Grandfather? I am not a teacher, Scorpion. I'm White Thunder. I only have seventeen summers."

"You are a teacher, and you teach by example. You are a coyote teacher. All of the slaves are starting to call you Grandfather, at least all of the slaves that work at the crushing floor or in the mine. We don't see the slaves at the smelter very often, so we don't know what they think."

Well, maybe I was a teacher, and maybe I wasn't. What good did it do to be a teacher if you were about to die. Still, our lives continued into the World of Shadows. Who knows what the Spirit World would hold?

• • •

Chind was also willing to go into the mine with me, so that morning we followed a guard into the mine and descended into the Underworld, candles in hand. The task of the guard was to show us our duties. There were guards occasionally in the mine, making sure the slaves worked, but the majority of the time the guards stayed outside.

We were shown the mine, such as it was, and shown our duties. Then the guard watched as we took out the first few loads. Since the Spanish had had slaves working the mine for three years, I expected a much larger hole. It wasn't a chasm to the Underworld after all, it was just an oversized cave and much less scary than I had anticipated. But the work was harder than anything I had ever done.

I had almost given up on working myself to death, but there

was something new that fascinated me: I was enjoying seeing my strength increase—not that it mattered much. Still, what would Towhee think of my new self?

Hour after hour, day after day we hauled the heavy loads of ore. Scorpion, Chind and I became an efficient team and genuinely liked each other's company.

One day, not as deep in the mine as you might think, a slave discovered a vein of ore that was so rich we wondered if it was pure gold. "Grandfather," he said to me, "if the Spanish find out about the rich vein, they will go crazy with greed."

"Not only that," I replied, "but they will make more Indians slaves, and it will be a never-ending process. Can you hide it from the guards?"

"Maybe I can for a little while, but eventually they will find it."

"Hide it then. It'll give us time to figure out what to do next."

• • •

The debris heap from the mine was growing larger than the Spanish had anticipated when they created the mine, and was beginning to encroach on the tiny stream. The guards had their camp located down by the smelter, blocking all exits from the mine. Most of us slaves slept farther up the stream from the guards. The guards had placed us there on purpose, so that they could more easily watch us and keep us within musket range. Between our camp and the guards' camp was the sludge debris pile. Repeatedly, the guards assigned slaves to clear out the steam so that water could flow to their camp and the smelter. It was ironic that while the Spaniards had the commanding camp, they had the worst water.

The guards also had a lack of personal hygiene, at least that is the way we slaves saw it. When we aren't captives, we Apaches take frequent sweat baths, cleansing our bodies from the inside out. It's a religious thing with us. After a good sweat bath and a dip in the stream or roll in the snow or sand, your body is cleansed.

As slaves, we sweat as much as we would in a sweat bath. Then at the end of the day we rinse our bodies and we are cleansed. But the guards never bathed, as far as we could see. They just perspired in their thick layers of clothing and let the perspiration dry. They smelled like stale sweat and other body odors. So when they started getting sick, we Apaches weren't surprised. But we wondered if they were getting ill because they had offended Ysun by not taking care of their bodies or if it was the bad water they were drinking. Or maybe they offended Earth Woman or the God of the Underworld by encroaching into their domain.

Sick or not, the guards still watched us, but they were clearly losing ground. Their faces were pale and their lips thin. The guards with the whips were less likely to expend the energy to use them—more likely to stand back and let us slaves do the work.

As the guards began to loose their threat, the slaves obviously began to think about escaping—that was plain enough for me to see. Of course the guards weren't dumb, and they could see it too. Sometimes they discussed it amongst themselves, and knowing that none of the slaves spoke Spanish, weren't careful to make sure that no slaves were around.

"Delgadito gave orders to kill half the slaves," one guard informed a second. "With so many guards sick, we can't guard all of them, and we can't take the chance of them telling others where the mine is located. This is the richest mine, but its location is kept such a secret that not even those that bring in the supplies know where the mine is." I had noticed that when supplies arrived, Cat Whiskers went down to the desert floor with a small handful of guards for the supplies. We never saw the teamsters that drove the teams across the desert.

The last statement about killing Indian slaves so that we couldn't tell where the mine was located totally baffled me. We Apaches have known where the yellow metal was all along. If we had wanted it, we would have mined it. Still, the Spanish didn't think like the Apaches.

The two guards drifted away and I was left to mull over their words.

The next day dawned, dark and angry. It rained on and off all day, and when evening came the storm grew even worse. During the day, it made cool and rather pleasant working conditions for the slaves. Yet we were in the mountains with lightning skipping over the ridges and bouncing off the rocky places.

I guess that all Native Americans fear lightning, or at least are very respectful of it. The Spanish would be too, if they had the sense to be. Our guards figured we should work, lightning or not. So despite their illness, they kept us working and had their hands full keeping everyone in line.

The guards were a little grumpier than usual, and a little mouthy too, within their own language. As I worked, I listened, trying to hear their plans as they talked. At last I heard what I wanted to hear. Two guards, ignoring me because they didn't expect me to know Spanish, were discussing Delgadito's orders.

"Delgadito has assigned a squad to take the less productive slaves out, one or two at a time, and knife them," one guard murmured, a note of disgust and complaint to his voice. Clearly he didn't feel well and wanted nothing more than to return to his camp and lie down.

"Why all that bother?" asked the second guard. "Why not

just turn our muskets on them and get it done in one move. It will save time and send a message to the remaining prisoners to work harder."

"Because we don't have enough muskets for all that. It would leave us with empty muskets when we needed them primed and ready to fire the most."

"When will the death squad start? I would like to be on it," said the second guard, obviously feeling more feisty than the first guard.

"Go see Delgadito. He is organizing it right now, and they will probably start in the morning."

• • •

This was it. At least some of the slaves' days as a slave would come to an end. I thought about it as I worked, and the more I thought the angrier I became.

"Why not go out in a blaze of glory?" I asked, borrowing a phrase from the guards.

"What did you say?" Scorpion said as he pulled the ore wagon.

"Oh, I was just talking to myself."

"It sounded interesting."

"I overheard the guards say that Delgadito was organizing a death squad to kill the weaker slaves. Apparently they fear that we will rebel. The guards are all sick, you know."

"Oh, I know. But how could you overhear the guards? They don't speak our language."

"I can understand Spanish," I replied.

Well, that stopped him in his tracks, and he just gapped at me. When he finally spoke, it was slowly and deliberate.

"You really are a shaman."

"No, I just guessed at what they were saying for so long

that I learned their language. Guessing what they were saying took my mind off my aching muscles when I was trying to work myself to death."

"Everyone has been talking about the guard's illness, waiting for you to do something."

"Me! Why me?"

"You're the grandfather and," he added watching my face, "probably a shaman, too."

"I'm just a slave that has seventeen summers."

"You may be just a slave that has seventeen summers, but you have the ears of the gods. No ordinary man can get us out of this. Some of the prisoners work in chains during the day, and they obviously don't have the freedom to help with the escape. And even those of us who don't work in chains during the day sleep with leg irons on at night."

"Yes," I replied, "I have been thinking about those leg irons, and I have an idea. It would take a while to get the leg irons off, but I heard one of the guards say that no chain is stronger than its weakest link."

"None of the links can be broken."

"Yes they can, at least they can be bent. Several of the links have opened up a little. If you put the partly opened portions of two links together in a cross, they will sometimes slip off. I tried it. The only problem is the sound of the clinking chains as we pull them through the loops on each slave's leg irons. For that we are going to rely on the gods."

"So you do commune with the gods."

"Talking with the gods is another matter. According to the shaman Kokopelli, you only really commune with the gods when you follow Quetzalcoatl," I explained.

"I don't understand. He's an Aztec god."

"I don't always understand, either. But apparently he is also the son of Ysun, and a great teacher of peace. But regardless of who talks with the gods, I noticed lightning to the southwest the last time we took a load of ore to the crushers. If we timed the threading of the chains with the roar of Thunder Bird, we could free ourselves. Of course we would still have on our leg irons, but we could take them off later."

Word spread, and that night the slaves that considered themselves the most apt warriors slept where the weakened chain links were usually located. As the guard threaded the chain through the loops on each prisoner's leg iron, the guard appeared sick and feverish. Clearly he lacked enthusiasm.

We were all lined up under an overhang to avoid the weather. We slaves didn't particularly like our location during thunderstorms as lightning wanted to dance over it. Placed against the overhang were boughs and cacti which formed a crude, elongated shelter. It also kept our movement secret from the eyes of the main camp an eighth of a mile or less down the draw.

"I wish I had my turquoise bead in my hair to protect me from the lightning," Brown Horse whispered. To the Navajos turquoise has a religious significance.

"Cat Whiskers could use a whole turquoise necklace," Chind muttered dryly in reply. As everyone cast him puzzled glances, he added, "to protect him against White Thunder."

The thunder claps seemed to be rolling into the distance. The storm seemed to be in a lull, which was not a good sign.

Having made sure we were secure, the guards moved off to their camp, leaving two sentries, one at each end of the overhang. Men usually stir slightly before they go to sleep, so we knew that a little rattling of the chains would initially be expected by the guards. Taking advantage of that, I immediately started fingering the loops and soon located two that had fairly wide spaces. Putting the spaces together and applying a little pressure, they easily slipped passed each other, effectively breaking the chain. Coughing three times, the signal that the chain was broken, all the prisoners quietly waited, some holding their loop in readiness of the thunder clap.

But the thunder clap didn't come. Indeed, the storm seemed to be dying out. So we'd have to thread the chain through the loops the noisy way. Though doing our best to keep the noise down, it was just a matter of time until it attracted the attention of the guards.

Having heard a noise, the guards lit a torch and entered the shelter simultaneously. It was their last sentry walk, because as each guard entered the shelter, one from each end, he was promptly relieved of his torch and his life, in that order. It was painless and clean, just a quick snap of the neck, Apache style, and it was all over.

• • •

I don't like to fight at night, neither did the three Navajos. It's not just a preference, but it's a religious thing with Apaches. There are spirits walking in the darkness into whom we don't want to collide. Neither do we want to lose our own life in the darkness because we don't want our spirit to get lost on its way to the World of Shadows. Still, when you have to do it, you have to do it. And there is nothing like years of being a slave to convince us that it was time to move. Of course, the Spanish knew of our feeling about the darkness, so they rested easier at night knowing that night fighting was not very likely.

We moved into position in a mountain rainstorm. The guards were all huddled in their shelter escaping the rain, venturing out only for the change of guards. We picked them off as they made their way to our overhang to meet the man to whom they were to relieve, but other than that we waited for first light. And when first light came, several Apaches stole into each shelter and took prisoners.

It was a great and glorious day for us slaves, as we were now free and in command. Once again we were the dreaded Apaches. Before I knew it, the prisoners began stripping off the guards' clothing and various forms of Apache torture were started. That wasn't to my liking, so I endeavored to reason with my fellow tribesman, though clearly they knew nothing of the teaching of Kokopelli.

"What is this?" I asked, half-demanding, half-yelling as I walked amongst the prisoners, kicking out the low fire which had been placed under Cat Whiskers. Naked as the day he was born, Cat Whiskers had been strung upside down over the fire and skinning knives were being selected.

"We are exercising our right to torture our former tormentors, Grandfather," a warrior innocently replied.

"And did your tormentor torture you?" I asked.

"Well, no. We were all beaten with whips as if we were horses and made to work as a slave, but we weren't tortured."

"Then you may beat the Spanish with whips, and you may take him to your village as your slave, but you may not torture him."

"That is strange teachings for a shaman," a stocky warrior said.

Turning to him, I said, "I may have strange teachings, but I am convinced that they are correct teachings."

"I had my toes cut off," another warrior spoke up. His name was Jer-On, and it was said that he could run from sunrise to sunset without stopping, covering more distance than a horse. The Spanish had cut off his toes so that he wouldn't run away.

"Is the guard who cut off your toes here, Jer-On?"

"Yes, he is over there. They were about to start a fire on his stomach before you approached."

"If it will make you feel better, you may cut off his toes. But you must cut them off quickly, with one blow of the ax, the same as he cut off your toes."

"Then what can we do with the prisoners?" Scorpion wanted to know.

"Unless you want to take them back to your village and make them slaves the way they made you slaves, let them go."

"But they're not good for anything as a slave. They can't plant corn, they can't cure hides, and they stink. What good are they?"

"You have a point there," I grinned. "Maybe you better let them go."

The prisoners were cut loose and given some of their clothes, but that was all. All of their possessions had become the property of some former slave. Fact is, the prisoners were even allowed to walk freely among us as we set to the task of removing leg irons and attending to the needs of the slaves that had worked at the smelter. Those at the smelter hadn't been part of our group and didn't even know of our uprising until we freed them.

The freedoms of the former guards were beginning to irritate the Apaches, and I wasn't sure how much control I had. "Round up your men," I said in Spanish to Cat Whiskers, "And take them to the overhang where they will have a little more safety."

Shocked, Cat Whiskers looked up so quickly you would have thought he would snap his neck. "I didn't know you spoke Spanish!"

"It never pays to underestimate your enemies," I replied with a grin.

My next job was that of removing the leg iron. I didn't intend to be the main man in removing the leg iron, but was just trying to do my share. But after I removed my own leg iron, I was soon wrapped up in the joy of the former slaves as their irons came off.

"Let's put the irons on the guards," someone said. The first time I heard it, it was funny, but afterwards it took on a more vindictive meaning.

"No," I replied every time it was mentioned. "Just leave them alone and you go home to your families, happy to be free."

One man was gathering up the legs irons. He was not one with whom I had spoken, and I paid him no mind. But in time I learned that he had taken the irons to the overhang where the Spanish guards were. His intent was to put them on the guards and make them walk back in a chain line to Mexico City or wherever they came from.

"Scorpion!" I called when I heard of it. "Find out who is bothering the Spanish guards, if you can, and see if you can get him to take whatever loot he wants and go home to his home village. There has been too much hate already. Besides, if the guards were chained together, it wouldn't take them any time at all to find a rock and warp one of the chain links enough to free everyone, same as we did."

Scampering off, Scorpion discovered it was one of the slaves from the smelter. He shooed the fellow away, convincing him that it was time to forget about the guards and start his long walk home to his family and friends.

It was late afternoon when Jer-On came to me as I was helping remove the last of the leg irons. "The Spanish have all been killed," he said, almost apologetically.

"What!" I demanded. "I thought they were in the overhang!"

"As near as I can tell, some figured you were going to chain them together in the overhang and leave them there to die. Others argued that you were saving them for some sadistic form of Apache torture. Regardless, they decided to make a run for it." We hadn't made any such plans, but even if we had, it would not have included torture. As far as chaining them together and leaving them to die, in time surely they would have been able to open up some of the links and free themselves before they died. I noticed that the chains weren't made of especially strong metal.

"Why didn't the men just let the guards go? Didn't I tell everyone to leave them alone?"

"We didn't do it. The slaves from the smelter did it. They knew you gave orders to leave the guards alone, but you are not a chief, and they do not know you as a grandfather or shaman. To the shelves from the shelter you are just another former slave. Still, they did not torture the guards; they just killed them."

The former slaves from the smelter departed, going their separate directions. Most of the other Apaches as well as the three Navajo stayed to help me wipe out evidence of the mine. There was a stack of gold bricks as high as a man's head, but no one wanted them except for the three Navajo. "Our people make much jewelry," said Kayenta. "We can use a little gold, though turquoise and silver are much more valuable to us than gold. But we don't want much because it is heavy and we are a long way from our home."

So Kayenta, Chind and Brown Horse took what gold they wanted to carry, and the rest of the gold was placed back in the mine. Our people have known where the gold was all along, and the Spaniards didn't need to know.

"Someday," I said in a rare moment of prophecy as we each departed our separate way, "this will be called an Apache massacre, and these mountains will be known as the Superstition Mountains. Many people will look for the yellow metal, but the only person that will find it will be he who uses the skills and has the vision of an Apache shaman."

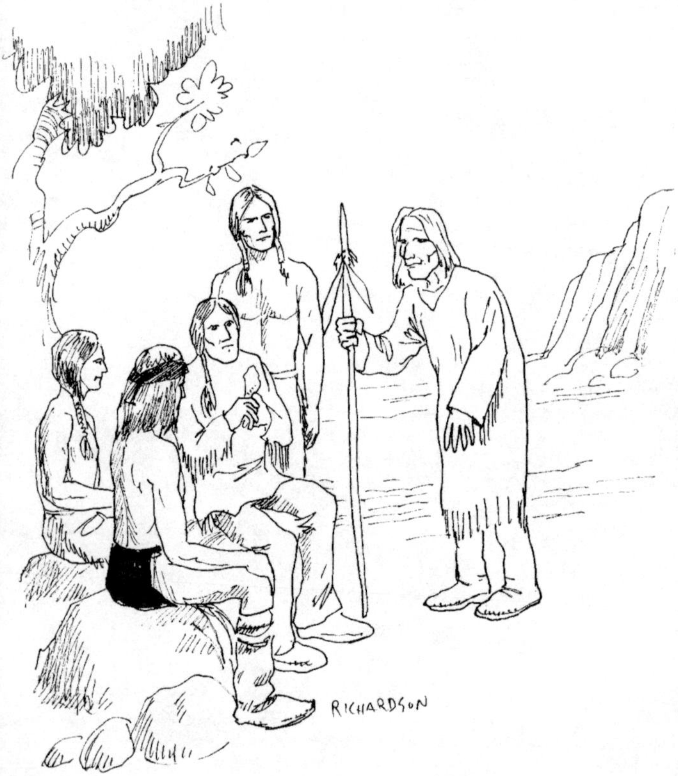
RICHARDSON

Excitement Was High

The desert was blooming in all its glory and the washes ran full as we made our way east. The sun was trying to reclaim the desert, making up for lost time as the desert steamed. The noisy wrens were doing their bird-jabbering in the cholla and enjoying the insect feast that always follows desert storms.

A large group of us had gone south to the lower desert and turned east to accommodate members of the Mescalero band whose villages were far to the east. Some of them had amputated toes, so the usual Apache trot was out of the question. The Navajo appreciated us foregoing the Apache trot as their tribe was not the runners we Apaches are. Not that the Navajo don't run, but an eighteen hour run is not something they are accustomed to. The Navajo stayed with us because making their way through Apache lands is not the safest thing for a Navajo if they should run across a mischievous band of Apaches. Generally speaking, only traders and shamans can freely travel through other tribes territories, and even that is isn't without risk.

Excitement was high for all of us to reach our homes and see what had befallen our families in the moons or years we had been in slavery. We were actually going home, something we figured would never happen. For some, there was the ever present ominous worry knowing that wives surely had to remarry in order to survive and children had grown up without their father.

Though we wanted to travel fast, out of necessity and a desire for food and safety, we stopped to make bows and arrows when we found appropriate willows. Everyone gawked at the peculiar Navajo style of using a bow and arrow. They held the arrow between the thumb and forefinger, but the bowstring was drawn with the second and third fingers. Surprisingly to us Apaches, they could hit what they aimed at. Our arrows didn't have stone tips, but were only wood. Neither the Navajo nor Apaches are big on making arrow heads; generally we trade for them, though there is a band of Apaches farther south that makes really good arrow heads.

• • •

Kayenta, Brown Horse, Chind and I left the rest of the group the morning of the fourth day and turned our faces north. The hanging valley where my people lived was only a few days' travel north. After the Navajo left me, it would take them another week to get home because they had to avoid bands of Apaches.

Crossing low mountains we came face to face with a deer, and it was there that the Navajo showed their skills in hunting without flint-tipped arrows. They ran the deer in relays, each taking up when the other got too tired to run. When the deer was so tired it couldn't run anymore, they suffocated it to death. We skinned it out with a piece of obsidian for a knife, and did a fair job of it, too.

Gorging ourselves with meat, we filled our stomachs really full for the first time since becoming slaves. We found that we couldn't eat much because our stomachs refused to stretch as they used to. So we paused to dry the remaining meat, which dried quickly in the hot sun.

Sitting by a trickle of water while the last of the meat was drying, we were surprised to see a man approaching. His stride was familiar to me, though I couldn't recall exactly who the stride belonged to. As he neared, coming from behind a juniper into full view, it was clear that he was none other than Kokopelli.

Maybe my actions told Kayenta, Brown Horse and Chind that someone important was approaching, or maybe it was the mere presence of the shaman as he advanced. He had no pack, no knife, no bow and quiver, nothing to survive on, yet he looked fed and nourished. Not dressed in the usual summer dress of an Apache— clout and high-topped moccasins— he wore a fiber dress typical of ancient shamans, and carried a shaman's feathered staff.

"He is Kokopelli," I whispered to my Navajo companions. I had told them much about the shaman and knew that they would know him by name.

"I know him," Kayenta observed. "He has been in our village teaching the women how to plant the blue corn in the most fertile places. He didn't have the flute that you have been telling us about, and I didn't know his name until now."

"I am sure he has a flute somewhere; I have never seen him without it."

"When he was in our village, he didn't have a flute, either," Brown Horse put in. "I have seen many drawings of him and he is always pictured as a hunchback, but I have never seen him pictured with a flute."

It amazed me that Kokopelli had made it all the way to the Navajo villages. He surely gets around.

Kokopelli approached without a word as one might expect of a great shaman and seated himself in front of us, as if readying himself to teach. We responded by seating ourselves in front of him, awaiting his words. But before speaking, he pulled out his flute and played a melody, putting us all in a reverent mood. Melody completed, he reverently tucked his flute away.

"Kayenta, Chind, Brown Horse, and White Thunder," he began, shocking us by calling us all by name. Surely he was a greater shaman than I had given him credit for. "You have all distinguished yourselves well in your year as a slave. You can be proud of your accomplishments."

"How do you know all of our names?" Brown Horse wanted to know.

"I make it a point to know the names of all warriors that show mercy and kindness to others, and that demonstrate that they are ready to be taught the ways of Ysun and Quetzalcoatl."

"But we haven't accomplished anything, Kokopelli. We have lost a year of our lives and our wives are probably remarried. We have helped no one."

Kokopelli looked me in the eye but it made me nervous so I watched his mouth. He touched the corner of his mouth with the tip of his finger, and then moved the finger to the corner of his eye. By that I knew that this was to be a soul-to-soul conversation with no eye-to-mouth conversation. But Kokopelli was the teacher, the shaman, so I followed his directions.

"You are taller and your shoulders are much broader, White Thunder. Your muscles are as solid as if they were iron, and as long as you never lie they will always sustain you in combat. You have shown compassion to your fellow slaves, not unlike Quetzalcoatl himself would have done had he been in your moccasins. You accepted your captors without hate and you even learned their language, and used it to try to help them. You were sold as a boy to the Spaniards, but are returning as a man."

"But what about my wife, Kokopelli? What about Towhee? Is she still mine? Has she remarried?"

A smile crossed Kokopelli's face, a beautiful smile that warmed my heart. But when he spoke, his words were serious.

"Towhee has had her struggles, but her future is up to you, White Thunder. Even now she sits at her wedding feast with Sieber."

"That can't be!" I jumped to my feet. "I love Towhee and I don't want her to go to Sieber. Besides, he and Shi-Be sold me to the Spanish, so I should hate him." Only then did I realize that I was standing, and quickly seated myself.

"It is only the second day of the wedding feast, White Thunder. If you make it to your village before they enter the wedding lodge tomorrow night, you can claim your rightful place beside your wife."

"But I can't possibly make it. It is two days run to the village and I have not run in a year. I have no moccasins to protect me against the thorns of the cacti and I am naked, save for this leather clout that I have worn all year."

"It is only a day's run if you strike off across the canyon

and run some at night."

"But Kokopelli, the canyon is lined with cliffs. And to run at night is risky. There are things in the night to trip a man."

Kokopelli rose to his feet as a sign that he was ready to depart. Yet he stood there, an obvious indication that he had departing words.

"If you want Towhee, White Thunder, you will do what is necessary to reach the village before tomorrow night. Commit the safety of Kayenta, Chind and Brown Horse to my care and take no thought of the spirits who inhabit the darkness, for they won't harm you. Trust in the god that made you and Towhee, for she loves you. But if you slacken, you won't make it."

"But Kokopelli—" I began again. My words were to his back because even as I began to protest my inadequacies, he was departing. There was no protest that I could make. Clearly, Kokopelli thought I could make it.

• • •

A red-tailed hawk circled over head, engaged in his evening hunt. As he passed between the sun and me, he cast a shadow that flickered across my path. I took it as a warning from the gods, a warning to make speed but to be careful not to trip or judge my route unwisely.

There were no good-bye words between my companions and me. They had heard Kokopelli's counsel and knew my mission. The nearest thing to a good-bye came from Chind who pressed a crude pouch of jerked deer into my hand and rested his hand for a moment on my shoulder.

I left at an easy trot with the sun two hands high in the clear evening sky, taking nothing with me but Chind's pouch of jerked deer. Ahead of me was a canyon, deep and ominous;

maybe it was a half-mile deep, maybe not, but it was deep and any route down would be long. Much time could be lost in the canyon if I chose a dead end path. At the bottom was a wide river that was swift running and strong this time of year. At night the canyon would no doubt be dark and scary, taboo to any self respecting Apache. In the darkness strange spirits lurk, but Kokopelli had said not to fear them, something easier said than done.

Falling into the rhythm of an Apache runner, the easy left, right, left, right of the pace came back to me. My muscles were still there, somewhat toned from the Spanish gold mine as I used my back and legs to push the ore wagon. Left, right, left, right—my breathing was matching my pace, but why shouldn't it? After all I had only been running a short time; by tomorrow at this time the breathing would be much harder.

I had been a year without moccasins and the soles of my feet were doing the job that Ysun created them to do. Rocks, cacti, sand, whatever, I picked my route carefully, making the best time I could. It was an impossible task I had set for myself, yet if Kokopelli thought I could do it, I did too.

Yuccas dotted my route and an occasional ocotillo and century plant got in my way. As I climbed higher, the junipers blocked my route, but at least when I rubbed against the junipers they didn't leave thorns. It was an easy climb: sandstone and limestone that occasionally gave way to stretches of granite and felsite. Sometimes brown, sometimes red, the soil was generally nothing to rave about, and surely not the kind you wanted to plant corn in. Generally the top was very slightly crusted over a powdery bottom layer. Thorns and thistles, they all got in my way, but still I ran.

Among the junipers was rabbit brush mingled with pungent sagebrush, and occasionally yuccas and century plants pointed to the sky. Jackrabbits darted first this way then that, their long ears looking like antlers.

The sun had moved a hand lower in the afternoon sky when I reached the canyon, granddaddy to them all except maybe the huge one far to the northwest in Navajo country. Steep cliffs and long drops, the canyon had them both. Yet I started down, following a trail of sorts. It was probably a trail made by the old ones, people that lived millenniums ago, but frequented by the four-legged tribes of today.

Down I went, racing the sun and making snap judgments at every turn. My mind seemed keen, my wind good, my feet alive.

It was a good trail, and going down was fast. The river was coming up, but so was a cliff that directly overlooked the powerful currents of the river. When I came to the cliff, the path seemed to end. I just stood there, searching and wondering. Surely the path wouldn't end here. Then I saw a fresh scar where a hunk of stone had given way and apparently fallen to the river below.

Below me was the river, but it seemed too large a leap. Quickly I reviewed my alternatives. The current was a long way below, but I must reach the village before Towhee got remarried, I didn't have much time. Again I judged the distance to the river and it didn't seem as great as before.

Acting before I lost my nerve, I took a big breath, then jumped. For a long moment I was a falling bird, suspended in space, then I parted the water and went under.

For an eternity I went down and thought I would never come back up. The current tore me at its will, and my lungs thought they would burst. When I finally bobbed up, breaking the surface and fighting for air, I was also fighting the angry current. Turning my concentration to the task of getting to the other side, I swam cross current, making slow headway. As I swam, I repeatedly cast glances to the shoreline for any type of a trail that might lead me to the rim. A deer saw me and wheeled around, crashing up a ghost of a trail. I gave the supreme effort as I was swept past the trail, but when I reached the shallows I grabbed a willow and pulled myself up. Then I waded back up the shallows that lined the edge of the river. When I reached the trail, it seemed strangely familiar to me.

For long moments I tried to place the trail in my mind, then suddenly I remembered. It was a trail from my youth, as I had wandered far and wide in my boyhood days. It wasn't far from our old arid home, the home we had before Kokopelli led us to the hanging valleys. It was a long way from our mountain home, but I knew exactly where I was. I also knew the route home.

Shadows had reached the lower part of the canyon, but the setting sun had made the rim an orange blaze sun. I was weakened from my long run and had swallowed much water. Yet I drank more—drank until I was as full as a tick.

The jerked deer meat that Chind had given to me was gone—where I lost it, I didn't know. Then I realized that it was tucked into my clout in front of me and I grinned with satisfaction at seeing that it was still there. In time I would need it.

Up the trail I ran, which wasn't much of a trail, but just a shadow of a route. The race was on to make as much distance as possible until the evening completely gave way to darkness. When it got completely dark I would have to hold up somewhere and wait for the moon to appear, hoping I could get a little sleep.

Soon I was drenched with sweat as if I had just stepped out of a sweat lodge, but I had made good time. No longer running most of the time, it was all I could do just to keep going up the steep canyon trail, using both hands as I climbed.

In the distance a coyote called, a mournful call that was answered by an equally lonely reply. Overhead a nighthawk darted for an insect. The nighthawks were particularly active; apparently they had a nest in the canyon.

Again I was running, or at least running when I could see the trail. I wanted to get out of the canyon before darkness took over, but didn't make it. I was more than halfway to the top, the way I figured it, but kept bumping against boulders, trees, and an occasional cactus. I looked for a place to rest until the moon appeared. Every shadow was scary, a potential spirit, but I set my jaw against my fears and went on.

There was a dip in the trail as I passed on the south side of a large boulder that held the heat of the day. The trail was fairly smooth and I dropped—dropped to the trail and lay still. Maybe I could see better to run without bumping into things in a few hours, but for now I had no vision and I needed rest.

Forcing myself to try to sleep, I allowed the weariness to drain from my muscles. Then I slept.

As I slept, I dreamed. In my dreams I saw a man dressed in a white shirt and leggings. They were both made of finely tanned white elk hides and he wore feathers that were topped in sky blue. In his hand he carried the feathered staff of a shaman.

"You have long sought your vision, White Thunder," he said.

"Yes," I replied. "I have sought it often, but it has never come."

"I bring it to you," he replied, handing me the shaman staff. "Take no other teacher unto yourself but Kokopelli. He will teach you all things, and you will teach your people."

The spirit handed me the shaman staff, and I clutched it to my chest as a sign that I accepted the call. Then he faded away and darkness closed around him.

• • •

When I woke, the moon was bright and full on my face. For a moment I lay still, mulling over my dream and listening to the sounds of the night, sounds made primarily by the insect tribe. At last, after all these years, I had received a calling from the spirits. My joy was so full that I broke into a chant of thanksgiving.

After a moment I looked to the stars and tried to judge the time. We Apaches don't generally use the stars to guide us at night as might some other tribes. At night we guide ourselves by landmarks, same as in the daylight. I looked at the trail such as it was. I would have to get a stick to hold in front of me to avoid bumping into whatever was in the deep shadows of night.

The chirp of a bird, faint and distant, caught my ears and I sat up straight in disgust. It was still full darkness and surely I couldn't have slept all night, but the bird chirp was real. Maybe it was the early morning insects that awakened the birds, I surely didn't know. Some birds wake early, in full darkness when there is still a quarter of the night left, and prepare to hunt predawn insects.

Throwing myself into the task at hand, I heaved to my feet and started out. When I entered the dark shadowed sections of the trail I had to slow to a walk. I would move with my hands out in front of me so that I wouldn't bump into things, but in the moon lit stretches I ran. In time I found a stick to hold in front of me because when the shadows held cacti from which I didn't want to get thorns.

Climbing out of the canyon was a slow process, as it was steep and many miles to the rim. Once on top I set my route along the most moonlit slopes. Not far off the path to the left I heard the scream of a deer in pain and knew that one of the night carnivores had made his kill. I had not heard the call of a wolf in chase, or yip of a coyote, so my guess was that the predator was a big cat, maybe a cougar or even a feisty bobcat.

There was quick movement of a shadow in a clearing. It startled me, but the movement came from the air and returned to the air. The silhouette of the bird indicated an owl. My guess was that a mouse had made a bad decision.

As the incessant chatter of the bird tribe increased, so did the grayness of the eastern horizon. Somewhere along the way I dropped my stick, as I was no longer blind in the shadows. The night feeding animals settled down for the day and the sun loving tribes of animals began to appear.

Hour after hour I ran, an easy stride that I hadn't used for a long time. The wind was in my face and hair, and my breath came easily. My muscles felt good—*I* felt good. I glanced at the sun and quickened my pace. Apache warriors can run all day, but usually not at this pace.

High, thin clouds set in, and as morning turned into afternoon the skies darkened. Afternoon thunderstorms are customary where I lived, and I welcomed the coolness. The wind from the south picked up and became quite stiff, blowing me along and cooling me even more.

When the first drops of rain came, I ran. When the heavens seemed to open up and drop torrents of rain, I ran. When the streams began to run red, I still ran. During the height of the storm, rain water cascaded down my body, cleansing it as might a dip in the stream after a sweat bath.

As the sun tilted precariously heavy in the western sky, I topped the ridge that overlooked the valley where our village slumbered. To my right was a tiny, cold stream, to my left were the lofty peaks that signaled home. Kokopelli had faith that I could make it, and I knew that if Kokopelli had faith in me, I could do it. And I did.

I paused for a dip in the water, letting my long hair flow with the current. I washed myself as if I were just emerging from a sweat lodge, and prepared to step into my future. My intestines seemed to leap into my chest for joy, but I was ready. All ready, that is, except for one thing, I thought as I stretched both hands to the sky. That one thing was to thank Ysun, Earth Mother, everyone. A squirrel looked at me and wrinkled his nose; a perfect messenger to take my thanks to Ysun.

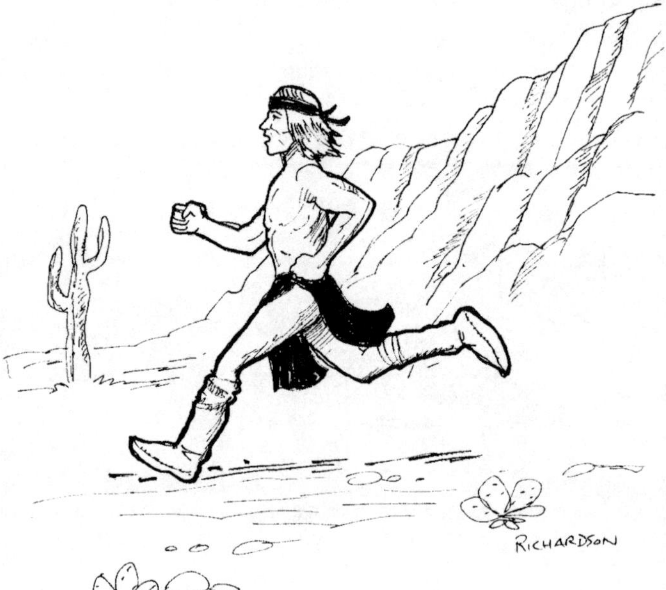
RICHARDSON

Regardless of the Drizzle

The open mountain slopes and moist meadows were glorious with the nodding blue bellflowers of the harebell as I carefully made my way down to the village. I was cautious because it doesn't pay to barge into a village where you obviously have enemies who are vindictive enough to sell you into slavery.

A light rain was falling, probably the last of the afternoon's thundershower offerings. The rain wouldn't last long, as it was already clear in the south and west, a rainbow bringing color to the mountains. Still, the villagers were probably in their lodges, escaping the final drizzle—at least they weren't in the open where I could see them.

Trying to remain unseen, I made my way to Towhee's lodge. She wasn't anywhere to be seen, at least from the outside. I didn't want to call her name and advertise my presence, so I slipped inside. It was empty, but on the man's side of the lodge were some clothes that I assumed belonged to Sieber, as he expected to move in, in a few hours. There was something else, too.

Baby clothes.

Reverent I touched the tiny clothes, realizing that she probably had my baby. After a few moments, I gathered myself together and slipped from the lodge.

• • •

My next stop was Mother's lodge. For that I had to backtrack and approach the village from a little different direction.

As I approached, I heard my mother singing. It was a working chant that the women sang as they worked. Keeping my back to the rest of the village so that they couldn't get a direct look at me, I slipped to the entrance. I didn't want to go inside unannounced, less my own mother would cry out, thinking I was an enemy.

"Hello, the lodge," I called softly, "this is your son."

"Come in, Nantan Lupin," Mother replied. It is almost unheard of for sons-in-law to go into the same lodge as his mother-in-law or even speak to her. But there always has to be exceptions, and Mother must have wondered about it.

As I slipped inside, I could see that Mother was busy grinding corn, making corn cakes. By the side of her grinding stone was a container of water which she used to wet down the corn as she ground. When she had a handful of wet, ground corn, she would form it into a little cake, ready for cooking.

She eyed me, questioningly.

"You're not Nantan Lupin," she observed. She studied me, and I just let her figure it out. A beautiful smile spread across her face as recognition set in.

"You are the ghost of White Thunder," she said. "Welcome to my lodge."

I was about to correct her when the babble of a baby turned my head. Stood against the aide of the lodge, a papoose peered out from under the hoop of a cradle board. Everything else forgotten, I just stared at the little tyke. Big eyed and a full head of silky black hair, was she Laughing Grass's papoose, Towhee's, or did she belong to someone else? Casting a questioning look at Mother, she read my thoughts.

"He is your son."

"Son?" I asked.

"Yes. His name is Koko, named for Kokopelli who instructed Towhee not to remarry until her son had seen four moons. He has seen four moons and four days."

I went to the boy and gently rubbed his little cheek with the back of my finger. He followed my finger with his mouth as if he thought it was something to suck.

"Don't spirits in the World of Shadows know what is going on in the physical world?" she asked. "Didn't you know that you had a baby?"

"Mother," I said, turning to her, "look at me. Look at me closely. It's me. I'm not a ghost."

Her fingers seemed to freeze in place and her eyes widened. From outside the lodge you could hear the evening songs of the crickets, and from Koko came a soft coo.

"But that can't be," she said. "You were struck by lightning and killed. Shi-Be and Sieber saw it, and Shi-Be even brought back one of your moccasins, partly burned, as evidence of your death."

I knelt down beside her and she touched my face gently, then ran her fingers through my hair. She melted into my chest and I folded my arms around her. From somewhere inside her came soft sobbing. I just held her close, wondering when she had become so small.

"If you didn't die, what happened to you?" she asked.

"If I tell you, can you keep it to yourself until I am ready to tell the village?"

"Yes, my son. I can keep your secret, but what is it that you want it kept so quiet."

"Shi-Be and Sieber, together, captured me and sold me to the Spanish as a slave. For nearly a year I have been working as a captive in the Spanish yellow metal mine."

"No, that's awful! Why do you not want to tell the village?"

"Because, Mother, kinship is strong among us Apaches. We must stand by our relatives even if we do not exactly agree with them. Half of the village are their relatives."

"True, White Thunder. Even you are related to his woman."

"I am?"

"Yes. If we go back far enough, we are probably related to everyone here."

"The situation is very delicate, Mother. I wish Kokopelli were here to talk with."

"He was here three or four days ago—just before Towhee accepted Sieber's pony as a marriage proposal. But you are right. You must use the wisdom of Quetzalcoatl, at least that is the way that Kokopelli would put it."

"You spoke of Towhee, Mother. How is she? I was to her lodge but she was not home."

"She is washing her hair in Yucca suds, preparing for her wedding night with Sieber. That is why I am tending my grandson. Her mother could not tend Koko because they are busy preparing food for the final day of feasting."

"You are making corn cakes, Mother. Are they for the feast?"

"Yes. There was much work for Butterfly Catcher—too much. So I am helping out."

"Mother," I asked, pushing her far enough from me so that I could study her face. "I have been gone for one year. Do you think that Towhee still wants me?"

She flashed me a curious smile and her eyes seemed to twinkle as she replied, "Ask the owl," which, of course, is the old Apache expression for, "Study the signs." As I thought of it, it really wasn't Mother's place to tell how Towhee feels, but her smile was encouraging.

The rain seemed to be letting up as we sat together in Mother's lodge. Periodically she glanced out the door of the wickiup, and at last she saw what she was looking for. Towhee was walking across the open area.

"Towhee will soon be here to nurse Koko," Mother said. "I must take these cakes to Butterfly Catcher's lodge to the cooking fire. Do you think you and Towhee can find something to talk about?"

Her mouth was turned up in a grin, and I knew I was home because I was being gently teased. Yet I truly was concerned and a little frightened that I might not make a good impression after so long away. I flashed her a worried grin, but said nothing.

Glancing past mother and through the opening to Towhee, I caught my breath. She was beautiful, maybe even more beautiful than when I married her over a year ago. She was a goddess, no less.

Stepping to the door as Towhee approached, Mother carried her cakes in a basket. "I must take these cakes to your mother's lodge, Towhee, to be cooked while you nurse the baby."

"Thank you, Mother," she replied, acknowledging that

Mother was doing a lot in making the cakes. In our culture, both of the parents of the husband and wife are called mother or father. The given name is never used.

Mother stepped out and Towhee stepped in. "Oh," she said at seeing me. "I didn't know that anyone was here."

"Towhee," I said. She froze, peering through the dim light of the interior.

"W-who is it? The voice has a familiar ring."

"Towhee," I said, standing to my full height. "It is I, White Thunder."

"Don't joke like that. White Thunder is dead."

"I am not dead, Towhee. I was captured and sold to the Spanish as a slave. A few days ago I escaped and was returning home when Kokopelli met me and told me that I must run across the canyon and even in the darkness, if I were to make it to you before the third day of your wedding feast."

"You are taller than White Thunder," she said, studying me, "and your shoulders are broader, much broader." She gently took me by the arm, leading me to the brightness of the entrance, but was surprised by my arm. "Your...your arms are larger than White Thunder's and you are much more muscular," she said suspiciously as she led me to the door.

"I have been a slave for almost a year, breaking rocks and working hard," I excused.

"It is White Thunder's voice," she said, pulling me around so that the light rested directly upon me, "I would know it anywhere."

Suddenly her eyes widened, as recognition finally set in.

"White Thunder, White Thunder, White Thunder!" She almost screamed, throwing herself into my arms. "White Thunder, it *is* you!"

Wrapping my arms around her I held her close to me and felt her body being racked with sobs—seems like women always cry. Like Mother, she seemed to have shrunk. I could feel the beat of her heart and the rise and fall of her chest.

"W-where have you been, White Thunder? I mean, you said you were a slave for the Spanish. Tell me more."

"I will, in time, Towhee. First I want to know about Sieber. This is the third day of your wedding feasts, so tonight you will slip away for a wedding night, if you want each other. Has he been good to you? Do you want him?"

I didn't ask if she loved him, as that is generally something not discussed a whole lot when choosing a spouse, at least not by Apaches. We talk about the man being a good provider, and being kind and sharing. Then we speak of the woman doing her household duties and being pleasant and tender. Love is something a couple develops over time.

"Sieber was kind and sharing, and provided my mother and me with much meat. He told of burying your body and of the heartache he felt at your death, you being a boyhood friend. He was sincere about it too, sincere about the heartache he felt at your death, his boyhood friend."

"He was?"

"Yes, he was. I know him, White Thunder. We were raised together, same as you and I were raised together, and I know he grieved for you."

I shrugged my shoulders. This was not the time to speak of Sieber's role in my abduction.

"He would make a good provider," she went on, "and I would have married him, but Kokopelli told me to wait until Koko had four months before I remarried.

"Clearly Sieber, and Shi-Be too, for that matter, have lied. I do not understand what is going on."

Holding her at arms length so that I could see her lips, I replied, "This is not the time for me to speak of Sieber and Shi-Be. I will speak of them only after your commitment to

Sieber is closed.

"I wish you for my wife, Towhee, if you will have me. I have this feeling for you, the feeling that the grandfathers call love."

At that she started to cry, and pulled herself close to me. "I have that same feeling for you, too, White Thunder," she said "I choose you as my warrior."

I just held her, but after a moment Koko decided that it was time for him to be nursed, so he started fussing.

"I have a confession, White Thunder," Towhee said as I still held her. Koko gave a demanding cry, more of a call to mother than a cry.

"A confession?" I asked, hoping Koko would hold off for a few more minutes.

"Yes. A confession."

"What is it?"

"I knew you would return, at least I knew we would be together in the next world. In consoling me, Kokopelli said we would be together. He said that if we were careful to follow his teaching about Quetzalcoatl, we would be together for eternity."

"For eternity? No one knows that."

"Kokopelli does."

"Well," I hedged. "Whatever Kokopelli says seems to always be true."

Again Koko started fussing, and this time he wasn't about to be put off. Towhee went to him and began nursing. Glancing out the lodge entrance, she commented, "I thought it would stop raining by now." Regardless of whom Towhee married, the villagers no doubt wanted the weather to clear up long enough for a dance.

"The young couples will dance in the rain," I replied, "and the other couples will take joy in the feast as they huddle in the council lodge."

Studying me as she nursed Koko, there was bewilderment in Towhee's eyes. "Though I don't know exactly what happened," she said, "I know enough to know that something awful took place, something that could break apart our village. How will you handle it, White Thunder?"

"I don't know, Towhee, but I will leave now and see you tonight. Between now and then I will be trying to get inspiration from the gods."

I bade Towhee farewell, and slipped into the gathering dusk. In the center of the open space at a huge fire, the feast was already in progress, regardless of the persistent intermittent sprinkles.

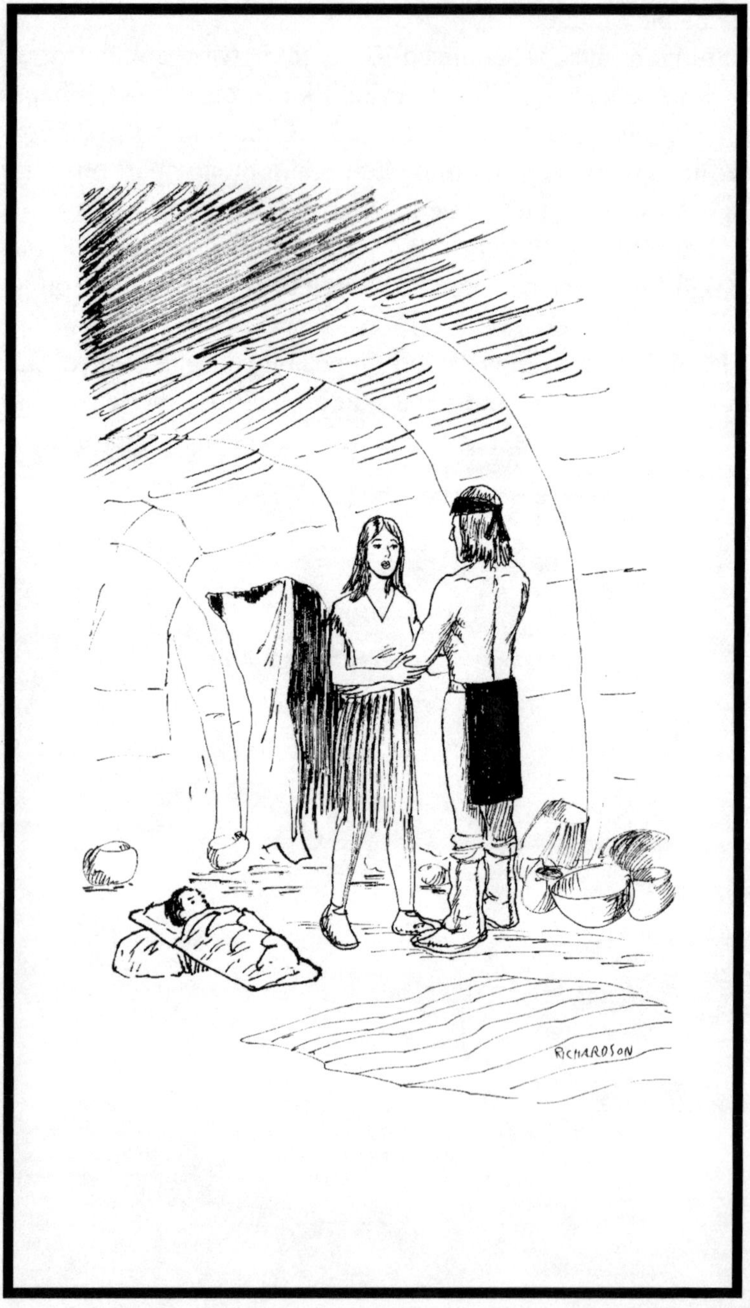
RICHARDSON

Outside the Firelight

The rain had almost stopped, yet all around us thunder roared and lightning flashed. Everyone knew it was not a good night for dancing.

The third night of the wedding feast was in full swing, such as it was, and dancers were setting a lively cadence, knowing the weather might open up into a downpour anytime. Still, they were in good spirits. All, that is, but the bridal couple. Clearly Towhee and Sieber were not getting along. They sat together in their places, but everyone knew something was wrong. It appeared that Towhee was calling the wedding off, or at least trying. But Sieber wasn't buying her explanation.

Having spent much time in prayer, or at least as much time

as I had, I returned to the village. Pausing in the darkness just out of the firelight, I surveyed the scene before barging in. I could only guess at what Towhee was saying. My best guess was that she was simply saying, "I'm calling the whole thing off," as I had not left her with enough information to give much more of an explanation. Of prime importance, we needed to recognize that Apaches stand by their relatives, and as weak as our village was, we couldn't afford to break it apart.

Was I scared? Yes. Clearly I was. I can face an enemy or wild animals, but things of a social nature scare me. Beside, even after pleading with the gods, I didn't know what to say. It was actually Shi-Be and Sieber's problem.

Suddenly I knew what to do.

It was Shi-Be and Sieber's problem, not mine!

I took a deep breath and blew it out slowly. It was time to let them know that I was home.

Not far away a bolt of lightning flashed and a woman screamed. We Apaches are terribly afraid of lightning, but generally people don't scream.

"What is it?" someone asked.

"Out...out in the darkness...White Thunder!"

"It didn't strike that close," someone said in disgust. White thunder is a phrase sometimes used for lightning.

"You don't understand," she defended herself. "When the lightning lit up the darkness, the ghost of White Thunder, Meatas's son, was standing out there."

The dancing had stopped as everyone stood around wondering and waiting for the next flash of lightning. No Apache—or Native Americans far as I know—takes the ghosts of the dead lightly. Ghosts are real, yet scary enough that Apaches fear the dead, even the dead shells of loved ones.

Well, I couldn't allow the villagers to think I was a ghost. It would only serve to make them afraid of me and would accomplish nothing. So I made my way to the fire. But as I was approaching, lightning flashed again. It was a brilliant flash that was even a little frightening to me. It lit up the whole mountain side and was followed almost immediately by a clap of thunder so close that it made the earth tremble. The villagers froze in their tracks as I was illuminated in mid-stride.

"Lightning flashed when I received my adulthood, and it flashes when I return," I said in an attempt at humor to set the villagers at ease. Though we Apaches love humor, they were apparently not in the humorous mood. Fact is, I began to realize, most of them were scared. No one cracked a smile, not even a grin.

Again the lightning flashed, striking the mountain just above us. It danced across the rocks in it's most frightening of all displays. The thunder clap that accompanied the lightning flash rocked us to our toes and sent children to their mothers.

Things were getting difficult fast, going from bad to worse. Clearly the Thunder God wasn't helping.

I recalled that back at the mine when the lightning was dancing near the overhang, the slaves were terrified, and it was hard to talk reason with them. The villagers were surprisingly like them. The usual sign for attention for my people is to raise both hands and wait for silence so that you can speak. So I raised both hands, and when they were silent, I spoke.

"Do not be afraid. It is just me, White Thunder, son of Meatas. I have come home."

After a few moments of silence, some commented, "Truly Meatas's son has miraculous powers. Even Thunder God obeyed him!"

"He is a ghost," someone else said, and the villagers started to murmur amongst themselves, giving opinions.

"I am not a ghost," I insisted. "I am White Thunder in the flesh."

How did I get myself into this situation anyway? Just when I was at the end of my wits to know what to do, Towhee came to my rescue by dashing around the fire and throwing herself into my arms. Wrapping my arms around her, I just held her, feeling the softness of her body and the gentle rise and fall of her chest.

After holding her for a few moments, Towhee slid her lips up close to my ear and whispered gently, "You're having as hard a time with the villagers as I was having with Sieber."

"Yes," I quietly acknowledged, "and Thunder God didn't help."

"Don't judge the gods too harshly," she replied, a tone of amusement in her voice. "And try to see it from the villagers point of view. They know you are dead, you are a hand taller than when you left, your shoulders are a whole lot broader, and your muscles ripple as you move, making you look like a god, not a person."

"What do I do next?" I asked.

"Leave it to me, my eternal warrior," she replied. Untangling herself from my arms, she turned to the villagers. "Friends," she said, "my warrior is home. Tonight he will join me in the bridal lodge. Please come and help me welcome him home."

Eskiminzin and his woman were the first to approach. "I don't know if you are a ghost or a person, White Thunder," Eskiminzin said, "but welcome home."

After Eskiminzin, many grandfathers and grandmothers lined up, led by Beyotas. Cautiously he grasped my forearm in the Apache version of a hand shake. Apparently he wasn't sure if I were man or spirit until he took my arm.

"It really *is* you," he said.

"Yes, it's really me."

"Thunder God took you a year ago and returned you today."

I must have sounded testy to the old man, but I didn't want him to get the wrong impression, so I replied, "Actually, I was not taken by Thunder God. I didn't die."

At that, Beyotas cast a questioning glance across the fire at Shi-Be, who stood there motionless, then returned his gaze to me.

" Shi-Be said that you were struck by lightning and that he buried you. When a warrior tells a story, Beyotas, is it the storyteller's right to improve the story on the next telling, or may another warrior improve it?"

"It is the right of the storyteller to improve his own story," Beyotas replied.

"Then let Shi-Be tell his own story," I said.

Softly, almost in a whisper, Beyotas said, "Does that mean that you are not going to call him out? The villagers will call you a coward."

I wondered what he would think if he realized how little I cared. After what I had been through, having some wimpy villagers call me a coward just didn't matter.

"Does Kokopelli fear being called a coward?" I asked.

"No. I don't think he does, though I have not heard anyone call him a coward."

"I don't fear it either, and I do not want to talk about Shi-Be," I replied. I glanced across the fire at Shi-Be. He didn't seem nearly as large as I remembered. He had grown older too, and appeared to be an old, paunchy man that was gaining years but not growing into a grandfather.

"You are beginning to sound like a grandfather, White Thunder," he observed, studying something in my hair.

"I try to learn the wisdom of you grandfathers, Beyotas,

and sometimes I succeed."

Other villagers greeted us, and when they asked where I had been I usually replied, "This is not a good time to discuss it." But for one particularly pressing grandmother I said, "I have been a captive, underground. I suppose I was in the near proximity of the Underworld. That's all I want to say." Her eyes widened and she pulled back as if I were an evil spirit.

"I can hardly wait to hear the story," Towhee whispered in my ear.

Most of the villagers had greeted us and dancing had begun. Across the fire and aloof from the group, Sieber held back. Catching his eye, I beckoned for him to approach, which he did timidly.

As he approached, Sieber looked like an overgrown whipped child. I couldn't think of him as my enemy, just as my childhood friend that I had done almost everything with. He stood there, obviously curious about what I might say. I just drew him to me and circled my arms around him like an old friend, giving him a man to man hug.

"Sieber," I said. "I never hated you, even when I knew I was going to die. I just remembered the good times we had while growing up and thought of the awful pressures your father must have put on you, even though I know the fault doesn't all lie with your father. And sometimes when I spoke with my fellow slaves, I forgot I wasn't talking to you and caught myself calling them by your name."

Suddenly his whole body was racked with soul shaking sobs as he cried on my shoulder. In the Apache culture, sometimes grandmothers and occasionally grandfathers will hug each other and cry. Nothing is said. They just cry. It is something people wouldn't expect in a culture that doesn't cry much, and you very seldom see it in young warriors such as Sieber. But I guess his soul had been racked so long with what he had helped his father do, that he needed to let it out.

Some of the villagers watched us from across the fire; others ducked their heads because they didn't want to see a grown man cry.

• • •

We had greeted everyone and I was tired, really tired. I had been running all day long and much of the night, covering more distance than a horse can run in a day.

"We're alone now," Towhee observed. "Shall we dance?"

I looked at the dancers enjoying themselves, then glanced to the council lodge where the food had been set up to keep out of the rain.

"Towhee," I said, "I am really too tired to dance. But I am hungry, really hungry. Let's get something to eat then retire to our lodge."

"That's what you always say," she replied. "You haven't changed a bit!"

Glancing at her to see if I was being rebuked, I saw a smile on her face and a twinkle in her eyes. "I, too, am hungry," she confessed as we started for the food. "But I would like to know about that feather in your hair."

"What feather?" I asked, searching my hair with probing fingers. My fingers touched a feather tied to some strands of hair and hanging down. I drew it into my line of vision and gapped in surprise.

It was a white feather with a sky blue tip.

About the Author

Boyd Richardson is an avid storyteller who helps his yarns come alive through vigorous research. His first three novels, *Voices in the Wind*, *Knife Thrower* and *Danger Trail* were published by Covenant.

Boyd says he does his best creative work while jogging. He is a marathon jogger, hiker, and backpacker. Raised in Salt Lake City, Utah and Snowflake, Arizona, Boyd filled a proselytizing mission to the East Central States, followed by a labor mission to the Northeastern Construction Area.

Boyd and his wife, the former Margie Powell of Lehi, Utah, have five "homemade" sons and one "imported" son, an adopted Korean boy. With a large family of boys, Boyd and Margie are deeply involved in Scouting (both are Silver Beaver Scouters). All six sons are Eagle Scouts. The older five sons are return missionaries, and the sixth son is serving a mission.

A graduate of Brigham Young University, Boyd works for The Church of Jesus Christ of Latter-day Saints. He teaches Primary, and serves in the Boy Scouts of America as a District Training Chairman.